SHORT CIRCUIT

WOLF HAAS

TRANSLATED FROM THE GERMAN
BY JAMIE BULLOCH

SHORT CIRCUIT

A NOVEL

HARPERVIA

An Imprint of HarperCollins*Publishers*

This is a work of fiction. Names, characters, places, and incidents are products of the author's imagination or are used fictitiously and are not to be construed as real. Any resemblance to actual events, locales, organizations, or persons, living or dead, is entirely coincidental.

HarperCollins books may be purchased for educational, business, or sales promotional use. For information, please email the Special Markets Department at SPsales@harpercollins.com.

hc.com

Originally published as *Wackelkontakt* in Germany in 2025 by Carl Hanser Verlag.

First HarperVia hardcover published 2026

Designed by Elina Cohen

Library of Congress Cataloging-in-Publication Data has been applied for.

ISBN 978-0-06-346916-7

Printed in the United States of America

26 27 28 29 30 LBC 5 4 3 2 1

CONTENTS

PART 1

OFF

Franz Escher was still waiting for the electrician when he finished the puzzle. He checked to make sure he hadn't deactivated the doorbell by mistake. Sometimes he forgot to turn it on again for days, because the coats and jackets hanging in the hallway covered the red light on the intercom that indicated whenever the bell was muted. Each time this happened he'd worry that he was beginning to become forgetful. But the intercom was working fine—he was just in the typical holding pattern you found yourself stuck in when tradesmen didn't show.

Although Escher wasn't an excessively impatient man, he didn't like it when he found too much time on his hands. Inevitably, he would start to brood. His brain would take up increasingly frivolous trains of thought such as whether his life would have turned out markedly different if he'd had another name. Even though it was more than thirty years ago that this name had occasioned the birthday present that would preoccupy him for the rest of his life.

He'd invited a few people over to celebrate his nineteenth birthday: his best friend, Andi, three schoolmates, the couple from the neighboring apartment with the thin walls (who he preferred to have over before they complained), as well as Daniela, his partner from the introductory seminar, and her enchanting roommate. Escher was proud at how casually he'd told Daniela's silent friend that she was welcome to tag along too, if she had nothing better to do. She was the main reason he'd invited Daniela, but with the sounding-casual routine he softened the blow of an anticipated rebuff.

But not only did this reserved individual come to his apartment that evening (Escher learned that her name was Martine with an *E*, because her mother was French), she handed the birthday boy a present swaddled in tissue paper.

After all these years he could still picture the scenario in greater detail than he cared to. He'd opened the package very carefully so that Martine wouldn't write him off as an insensitive brute, with enough determination to look suitably purposeful. After all, it was solely for her sake that the evening had been orchestrated. Escher's approach to even the simplest things in life was so overwrought that even a little birthday party had to be "orchestrated." And yet Andi had assured him that this half-French girl fancied him. "She's got a crush on you," were Andi's words. But Escher reckoned his chances of getting into this adorable creature's pants, even given the perfect combination of alcohol and good conversation, were 5 percent tops.

With a vigorous but not overly theatrical gesture, Escher released the birthday present from its wrapping, aided by a Stanley knife whose sharp blade had severed the sticky tape without damaging the paper. Andi flashed him an enthusiastic grin and sent eyebrow signals of encouragement while nodding eagerly. As far as Andi was concerned this was the final proof that shy Martine had the hots for Escher. Why else would she have thought of such a nice birthday present? For the other birthday guests, too, it was a done deal: Martine was loveliness personified, and Escher's athletic build was undeniable. Moreover, it had been years since anyone had called him by his nickname, "Neanderthal," which he'd earned by growing all too quickly, and for having an untamable head of curls and high cheekbones. Even Escher's legendary sluggishness could be mistaken for profundity and discretion by someone with a hormonally distorted perspective.

"A puzzle!" he said with an idiotic expression, staring in disbelief at the box in his hands. He couldn't tell for sure if he was being made fun of. After all, he wasn't a little boy anymore—a nineteenth birthday party surely should have confirmed that. But he didn't let it show. Following the established rules for accepting presents, he managed to avoid sounding disappointed, embellishing his reaction with a note of surprised delight: "A puzzle! How cool is that!"

Martine, who frequently felt secondhand embarrassment, hoped that it would soon dawn on him, but Escher was slow on the uptake. Although he could see the disappointment in her eyes, he simply didn't catch on and to be on the safe side said again, "Cool! A puzzle!"

He wasn't usually so dense. On the contrary, he attended nearly every theory seminar on campus and was dreaded by his tutors as a merciless hair-splitter. If, however, he took interest in a woman (even decades later he knew the telephone number of Martine's apartment by heart) and was keen to appear in the best light, his IQ plummeted. With the box still in hand, he floundered. But he was alarmed by Andi's reaction—eyes flashed at him triumphantly, almost ecstatically, as he bared his teeth like a benign cannibal. In the end Andi's patience ran out and he gave his friend a nudge. Irritably, he tapped his index finger on the picture on the lid of the box.

"Escher!" he cried. "That's fantastic—an Escher!"

And finally, the penny dropped for Escher too. Martine had actually gone to the trouble of finding a birthday present that shared his name. The puzzle was a picture by his famous namesake, one of M. C. Escher's optical illusions where two hands bizarrely draw each other into being.

"That's so nice," Escher said. "One thousand pieces! Where did you find it?"

To make up for his faux pas he immediately emptied the puzzle onto the floor and urged his guests to assemble the thousand pieces with him. And because it was his birthday they humored him, but nobody went about it with as much enthusiasm as Escher himself. The celebratory dinner dwindled into a self-service buffet, including a number of exhortations to the guests not to smear the puzzle pieces with greasy fingers. Escher got so lost in the puzzle that he didn't notice the time passing and the first yawning guests leaving after midnight. In the end only Andi and Martine were left, crawling on the floor with Escher among the pieces.

But Escher didn't pay these last two guests much attention either. It escaped his notice that Martine, kneeling over the puzzle as it gradually came together, kept reaching for the remaining pieces in such a way as to ensure that her unmissable assets came between the gift and its recipient. She hovered over the picture like a bird of prey, and only a fool would have mistaken this for yoga. The hands she kept brushing were not those of the image, but the now well-proportioned hands of the birthday boy, handing him a puzzle piece or taking one from him. Escher, however, was only interested in the thousand-piece cardboard picture that was taking shape. Two hands drawing each other, an intensifying madness that, as more alcohol was consumed, approached the metaphysical.

Eventually Martine left in disappointment with Andi, and the following day Andi asked Escher if it was a problem for their friendship that he'd gone off with her.

"Well," Escher admitted, rather sheepishly, "that wasn't actually the plan."

Like most people, he wasn't going to miss out on the opportunity to feel unfairly treated.

But then he composed himself and shook his head. "Look. I'm happy for you," he said. "You know what? I finished the puzzle at half past seven. I've already ordered the other one!"

"What other one?"

"The one on the back of the box. *The Tower of Babel*."

For years *The Tower of Babel* remained his favorite despite many new acquisitions, only to be finally knocked off the top spot by *Madonna with the Long Neck*.

But he hadn't wasted any of his best ones today in waiting for the electrician. Not *Madonna with the Long Neck*, nor *The Burial of the Count of Orgaz*, nor *The Ten Thousand Martyrs*, nor *The Beheading of Saint John the Baptist*, and certainly not *Self-Portrait in a Convex Mirror*. As with your favorite songs, you had to be careful not to exhaust their appeal through overexposure. And so, the puzzle that lay finished on his parquet floor was *The Great Wave off Kanagawa*—his low opinion of this one boiled more down to the fact that it had only five hundred pieces than because the image had become clichéd. Maybe his choice had also been subconsciously guided by the painting's title. The *Great Wave* was somehow fitting for the electrician's visit, seeing as most power in the country was generated by water.

But now the *Great Wave* was finished and the electrician still was not here. "In the afternoon"—the woman on the phone hadn't cared to be more specific. This meant hours of waiting, supplemented by the nagging worry, growing by the minute, that the electrician wouldn't turn up at all and Escher would have waited in vain. To avoid becoming even more exasperated, Escher reached for the book he'd started the previous evening.

For a long time now he'd read only one type of book, though with a passion that almost matched his puzzle obsession. Anything about the Mafia—'Ndrangheta, Cosa Nostra, Camorra—he devoured them. Nonfiction, potboilers, academic works—anything he came across in this field he consumed more or less indiscriminately. He knew the notorious families better than his own, which barely earned the distinction. This latest novel was about a young criminal in Aspromonte whom the police had flipped. His testimony sent twenty-seven high-ranking members of the 'Ndrangheta to prison for years and decades. In return the police had promised to put him under witness protection and provide him with a new identity in a different country.

The first chapter, which Escher had read before going to sleep, was a devastating catalog of the violent acts the witness had described. From the start of chapter 2, Escher was terrified for the young detainee's life. His name was Elio, but the newspapers called him Pavarotti on account of how beautifully he was singing. He was due to be released from his high-security cell in four days, dispensing with his former identity forever. A new life had been arranged for him in Germany, that was the deal. It was the reward for his betrayal.

But as his new life drew closer, the greater grew Elio's conviction that he was going to be bumped off just before his release. Although he was in the most secure cell in the most secure prison in the country, he was certain he'd be executed. He knew how they worked. They had people everywhere. Police, prison, courts. It was obvious that they had to kill him as revenge for the twenty-seven bosses he'd ratted out.

Elio didn't even trust the German drug dealer the investigating judge had assigned to his cell to help teach him his future language. Not one bit. Sven, the junkie with the junkie's voice, was the only friend he had. Which didn't exclude the possibility that Sven might slit his throat one night. Sven shook so badly that he could hardly hold a spoon, but he might still be able to thrust a knife into Elio's stomach while he slept. Ever since the day of his release was decided, Elio had allowed himself to doze off only when there remained no doubt that the sleeping tablet had sent his cellmate into the deepest prison dreams. And Elio never slept without one hand on the toothbrush he'd fashioned into a shiv and hidden in the mattress.

The investigating judge had impressed on Elio that learning German from the junkie was a welfare measure and a great privilege. Maybe he was being serious. Over the years the judge had won the young witness's trust. Until the trial he'd done pretty much all that Elio had asked and smuggled into the cell everything his star witness wanted. Once he'd even shown him a photo of his orange Laverda 750, which he'd had since his student days in Rome. It was the same model that Elio's cousin Dino had been riding when they shot him at the traffic light. The investigating judge knew more about motorcycles than Elio could have imagined. The young inmate enjoyed these private conversations when he could briefly forget everything else. But once all the witness's statements had been documented in court, the judge's behavior changed. His visits became less frequent and his attitude toward the now redundant witness grew cold. He hadn't shown his face once over the past few days. *It's probably better for Falcone if I'm dead,* Elio thought.

Just as soccer players were given the names of past legends, the newspapers had baptized his investigating judge "Falcone," after the famous Sicilian Mafia hunter. In fact, it wasn't the newspapers that had come up with this nickname, but the mob bosses who owned the papers. The supposed honorary title carried an unmistakable threat. Soon everyone referred to him as Falcone, who in the great Palermo trial passed hundreds of sentences before being blown to smithereens by Totò Riina in his Fiat Croma, along with his wife and three bodyguards.

Elio woke with a start. He'd briefly nodded off while pondering the possible reasons behind the change in Falcone's behavior. He focused again on the book that was supposed to help him keep awake until Sven's snoring was loud enough. The book was a gift from Sven. It was in German and Elio deciphered it page by page with the help of a dictionary that Falcone had brought. The story was about a guy called Escher, like that other guy called Escher. Escher had been waiting hours for an electrician. When he rang the company in an attempt to get more information, he was simply put on hold. As he was listening to the music, getting used to the idea of spending the rest of his life like this, the doorbell finally rang.

"Elektro Janko," a man wearing a baseball cap spoke into the intercom.

The cap concealed the man's face on the intercom's video. Escher opened the door to his apartment and waited. Although there was an elevator, he heard him trudging up the stairs. When, head bowed, he reached the last few steps, Escher saw that the two words *Elektro Janko* were embroidered in red on the blue cap, one above the other. This design allowed the two words to share a large, single *O*. Within this circle they'd also put a lightning symbol, which so dominated the poor *O* that the human eye was capable of reading only *Elektr Jank*.

Maybe it was this clumsy embroidery that made the face beneath the cap appear so well-proportioned: a short, dark beard framing a strikingly pale face. The exceptionally beautiful dark eyes that peered seriously at Escher reminded him of the shepherds and saints in some paintings he had as puzzles. In a reserved but confident manner the visitor announced, "Hello. Elektro Janko. I'm here about the outlet."

He simply took off his shoes rather than inquiring at length whether he should. Then he followed Escher into the kitchen, where he was filled in. There was a loose connection in the single outlet above the work surface. Over time the ceramic plate had cracked in various places, eventually crumbling altogether. Escher had been living with this dangerous-looking setup for years and felt increasingly uneasy whenever he had to unplug anything. Because this was the problem: Several times a day he had to switch between the kettle and the coffee machine. But it wasn't until he'd discovered a loose contact that he'd finally decided to call in an electrician.

"Is it actually dangerous or does it just look criminal?" Escher quipped.

The electrician merely gave a slight raise of his eyebrows in response. Escher fancied he could detect a certain disdain in this reply, as if any explanation to a customer with an outlet like this was superfluous. But he also knew that he had a strong tendency to feel scorned, a quality he disliked in himself. And so he defended the electrician against his own judgment. He was an introverted, down-to-earth type. Didn't say much but did everything properly. There was also something elegant and unfussy about the way he opened his tool bag. Escher took to the man. He'd never been able to stand chatterboxes.

And, as Escher had recently discovered, reserve didn't automatically go hand in hand with the profession of a technician. The fat man from the heating service had bombarded him with tales about his private life. Wife! Lover! Hahahaha! Afterward the windbag, exhausted from talking, had forgotten to take away the dirt he'd scraped from the boiler. Escher himself had to dispose of the rust that had been left in the bin. The electrician was of a different caliber. He exuded a quiet competence. It was hard to guess his age. He was younger than Escher but he wasn't wet behind the ears.

"I expect your colleague on the phone already told you," Escher began, interrupting the electrician's silence. "I don't just need a new outlet. I need three here instead of one."

The electrician nodded and asked Escher where the fuse box was, but he was already looking toward the hall. Of course, he must know from experience where fuse boxes were normally found. Or he might have spotted it when he came in, beside the door, above the coats covering the intercom. Escher wondered why he'd bothered to ask. Maybe it was out of politeness, maybe the man felt too proprietorial if he immediately found his way around people's flats. After all, he wasn't at home here. Once the electrician had flipped the switch in the hallway he removed the rest of the old outlet and explained that in order to install a three-way outlet on plaster, it would have to be mounted and stick out from the wall.

"It won't look pretty," the electrician added, "but you'd have to have it chiseled out otherwise."

"Doesn't bother me," Escher said. "All I'm worried about is the loose contact. And that I keep having to switch plugs. Either the kettle is in or the espresso machine. You always need the one that isn't plugged in. And I've got a toaster too."

Nodding once more, the electrician got down to work.

To leave him in peace Escher went into the living room, leaving the door to the kitchen open. On the floor was Hokusai's *Great Wave*. The picture riled him. Even though he'd read the book *Waves: A Very Short Introduction* in English and now felt very knowledgeable about waves, he still remained mystified by the picture. Escher's frustration stemmed from his inability to comprehend the picture because it came from a different tradition. This made him hostile toward the picture itself. As he put the pieces of the puzzle back into their box, he heard the electrician's phone go off in the kitchen: a piece of downloaded music rather than a generic ringtone. Before Escher could identify the song, the electrician had already picked up. All he said was, "Yes, okay, fine. Understood. See you later."

Then it was quiet again. Escher lay down on the sofa and resumed reading from the point at which he'd been interrupted by the electrician.

At midnight it occurred to Elio that there were only three days until his release. Sven was sleeping but not deep enough. Shortly after two o'clock, when Elio was finally about to succumb to sleep, he heard footsteps echoing in the prison corridor. He froze as if he'd taken a dose of the suspended animation medicine the boss of bosses had used to escape from the highest security prison. The metal door opened with such a crunch that he found it hard to believe Sven could continue snoring away so peacefully. Elio's right hand gripped the toothbrush handle fused with the razor blade. A single man, wearing a full-face helmet, entered the cell.

The junkie snored.

Elio tried pretending to be asleep but he was too paralyzed by fear to manage a single deep breath.

The nocturnal visitor approached slowly, stopping by his bunk. In the darkness his white astronaut's head bent over Elio's face.

"Wake up, Elio," the helmet whispered. "It's me."

Elio was startled. He recognized the voice at once. What was the judge doing in his cell at this time of night?

"Falcone?" In a normal situation Elio never would have dared call the judge that. "What the hell are you doing here?"

Falcone had last visited him a week before, when he had informed Elio of the day he would be released to embark on his new life. What Elio couldn't have known was that this decoy date was yet another security measure. Just like Elio's suicide, which the guards had reported that night.

Falcone cradled another helmet under his arm.

"Put this on."

Falcone had insisted to those few in the know that it must be him who would transport young Elio to the station in Lamezia. He'd grown fond of his key witness over the past months and years. Not a single person was to be told the exact time. Falcone knew this was the only way he could get Elio out of the prison alive.

Clutching the helmet, Elio followed the judge out of his cell and exited the prison gate. Waiting right outside was Falcone's orange Laverda 750. Only when he felt the street beneath his feet and the night air on his skin was he finally able to believe that this wasn't a dream.

"Where are we going?" he asked the judge as he slipped on the helmet.

"We'll start with the cemetery," Falcone said. Elio clambered behind him onto the bike. He started the engine. Elio was surprised that the Laverda didn't blow up. The bike hadn't been rigged with explosives, and the engine was purring good-naturedly. Although the judge set off smoothly and was clearly a seasoned biker, Elio held on anxiously. After his prison stint, even the speed of a Vespa would have been too much for his nerves.

At the cemetery they wandered over to a small grave. Falcone led the way with his flashlight and eventually shone it on the inscription of a headstone:

ELIO RUSSO 5/2/1981–6/11/2002

"The eleventh of June? That's today," Elio exclaimed.

Falcone nodded. "You killed yourself," he said.

"How?"

"None of your business. It's a private matter."

"But *my* private matter."

"No, you're Marko Steiner."

Elio found it hard to part with his name. His grandmother had always said he was named after Helios, the god of the sun, because the sun never sets. And although the sun had set every evening, he liked this story. When Falcone turned off the flashlight, the name was still legible in the moonlight. The stars too seemed to have grown bigger during his three years in prison. It was the hour before daybreak, when the heat eased off slightly. Elio was dead and Marko Steiner alive.

The two helmeted cemetery ghosts stood by the grave a few moments longer, staring at the inscription. Then they crossed themselves and climbed back onto the motorbike. Gradually Elio became accustomed to the speed. He tried to make out the stone villages flying past in the darkness. It was the last time he would travel through this landscape that before now he had hardly ever left.

At Lamezia station the judge handed over an envelope with new papers.

"You're a year and a half younger now too. Which means you've recovered half of your time in the slammer," Falcone laughed.

Marko took off his helmet and gave it back to the investigating judge.

"I wish you the very best," Falcone said. "Your new life begins now. You're a good lad."

He briefly hugged his star witness, whose hair was flattened like the fur of a newly born calf. Then he sped off with a loud rumble.

Tickets were in the envelope too. Although the train was due to leave at 5:55 a.m., it was still on the platform at 6:15. Marko Steiner waited for someone to climb aboard and shoot him. At 6:30 the train still hadn't departed. Marko listened to the footsteps and voices outside and the slamming of doors in other cars. Hurried footsteps approached from behind, but the guy rushed past him without so much as a glance. By 6:40 still nobody had shot him. Eventually a voice blared out something unintelligible over the loudspeaker, and soon afterward the train left with a jolt.

No sooner had he relaxed a little than the conductor came into his carriage. Marko took the ticket from Falcone's envelope.

"Are you Marko Steiner?"

Marko felt a shudder when the conductor uttered his new name. He had a port-wine stain beneath his left eye that was almost violet.

"Why?"

"The ticket is made out in his name."

"Yes, of course," Marko replied, relieved.

"You can't sit here, Signore Steiner! This is first class!"

"Oh, I didn't see that."

"Didn't see? You have to go to second class!"

Marko picked up his backpack and went to sit in an almost empty second-class car. He nodded off briefly and was woken by a coffee seller staring at him with a cold-eyed gaze. For a split-second Elio thought it was Fausto Griglietto, but it soon dawned on him that Fausto was serving a life sentence in prison because of Elio's testimony. Fausto had two brothers who had evaded arrest. But rather than shooting him, the coffee seller was satisfied by the passenger's purchase of a *doppio*. Unsure of how to settle his racing thoughts, Elio took Sven's book out of the backpack and tried to read a little.

From the living room Escher listened as the electrician went about his business. He wondered whether to show his face, just to be polite. Before he could do this, however, the doorbell rang. He went over to the intercom and although he couldn't see anyone on the screen, Escher said, "Hello?"

It was probably a deliveryman or someone distributing flyers who'd tried all the buttons and was now in the building.

"Hello?" Escher said once more, looking at an image of the empty street. Maybe he should mute the doorbell to avoid any further disturbance?

Sometimes Escher pressed the peace-inducing mute button by accident when in fact he was trying to open the door. His finger would mistakenly hit the white button beneath the blue door-opener, deactivating the doorbell. Usually, he would catch his error at once when there came no buzz and the red indicator light flashed on. The slipup manifested not merely as the unconscious result of his desire to be left in peace, but also directly as a result of the system's deficient color scheme. The intercom was entirely white, apart from the door opener. That was blue. So, actually, it should have been really hard to hit the wrong button. *Foolproof*, the designer of the system had probably thought. This anonymous designer was Escher's nemesis. Sure, the entire box was white, which made the blue button impossible to miss. But this clarity was canceled out by a second idiosyncrasy. The flood of red light when the mute button was pressed imprinted itself on the mind even stronger. This double exception (blue door opener, red light beside the mute button) made it all the more likely that you might mix up the buttons. Often you would get to the intercom in a hurry that bordered on panic. To avoid missing the courier yet again, you had to rush to the intercom, suppressing a recurring fear that there might be an unpleasant surprise waiting for you at the door. In such circumstances it was easy to get your wires crossed between the blue and the red, and in your haste you'd push the mute button instead of opening the door.

But now it would have been a mistake to turn off the doorbell. The electrician might have to pop out to his car to grab something, and when he came back Escher wouldn't hear him buzz. When he hung up the handset he noticed the open fuse box above the intercom. Two black circuit breakers were out of line, flipped down rather than up. The electrician had switched them down with a *click*, shutting off the flow of electricity.

Maybe Escher was still thinking about the two intercom buttons. Or maybe it was just his general need for order, or the restlessness of his fingers, whose urge to press the door opener had not been satisfied. Or his brain, accustomed to one-thousand-piece puzzles, engaging in displacement activity after the measly five hundred pieces of Hokusai's *Great Wave*. Or maybe it was a combination of all these factors that caused Escher to absent-mindedly flip the two circuit breakers up.

At the same moment he heard a slight clatter in the kitchen. It was the laconic sound screwdrivers make when they fall onto a work surface. The loud thud did not carry to Escher's ears immediately, but only after a brief delay. This was how long it took for the electrician's body to slump onto the floor. Without shutting the white door of the fuse box Escher rushed into the kitchen and discovered the motionless body.

Although he had seen the circuit breakers flip down again with his own eyes right before the thud, he returned to the fuse box to check that this had really been the case. He didn't want to get electrocuted himself. Only then did he turn his attention to the electrician lying there silently. The cap lay beside his head. Two eyes stared lifelessly from his handsome face. Now it occurred to Escher who that face reminded him of. Not a shepherd or a saint, as he'd first thought, but *Portrait of a Man* by the painter Parmigianino, which Escher had assembled on so many occasions.

His attempts at resuscitation were rather half-hearted. He'd never been the type who thought he could raise the dead. The short beard, the mouth no longer breathing, now looked to Escher as though it had been glued on. He recalled the first-aid course he'd done alongside his driving test. The thing that had stuck with him most was that you had to be careful when performing chest compressions so as not to break the patient's breastbone, thereby finishing them off. Besides, he was convinced that the electrician was already dead. Breaking the dead man's breastbone seemed even more reprehensible than having actually killed him, which after all he had done unintentionally and (apart from the slight resistance of the circuit breakers) impalpably from a distance.

He left the body of the electrician in peace and contemplated his next steps. Who should he call? An ambulance? The police? Elektro Janko? And should he admit to what had happened? Or should he play dumb and allow the blame to pass automatically to the electrician? Was it conceivable that a professional electrician might forget to switch off the circuit breakers? It wasn't but, in view of the facts, it would be hard to deny. Nobody would suspect him of such inexplicable barbarity.

But he was also reluctant to lay the blame at the electrician's feet. Maybe it would create problems with the insurance for his wife. The wedding ring on his finger was prominent. Escher wondered what consequences might lie in store for him if he stuck to the truth. Maybe he would be put into psychiatric care. The fact that he couldn't be 100 percent sure whether the electrician had asked him to flip the circuit breakers up again, for only a moment, would definitely be used against him.

He didn't see why he ought to put himself at the mercy of the state's machinery all because of a tragic accident. It would be a cruel and unusual punishment for something he hadn't meant to do. And it wouldn't bring the electrician back to life either.

A sudden vibration wrenched him from these thoughts. Like a defibrillator, the mobile vibrated briefly in the breast pocket of the blue work jacket, where "Elektr Jank" was also embroidered. Absent a ringtone, Escher suspected it was just a text message. It didn't reanimate the dead man, but it did inspire Escher to get up. Everything went black briefly, as if he'd spent hours on the floor trying to keep the electrician alive. Propping himself on the windowsill, he peered out the kitchen window for a while.

His father had drilled it into him that in difficult situations you should never make a rushed decision. Count to ten, count to one hundred, count to one thousand. Wait until the following morning. The more difficult a situation, the more important it was to sit on it. Any calamity that ever was was only exacerbated by rash judgments and thoughtless decisions.

Escher was pleased that he remembered this advice now. To be able to think in peace, he turned off the bell and returned to the living room. His eye caught sight of the book lying open on the sofa. As a matter of principle Escher did not dog-ear pages in books, but there was not always a makeshift bookmark on hand. Usually, he would just leave the book face down at the page he was on, which meant that over time the binding grew saggier and saggier. He'd never regretted this wanton neglect before— perhaps the prick of conscience he was experiencing now bore some relation to the tragedy that had just unfolded in his kitchen.

In truth it was a shameful habit, considering that Escher

himself had published a book when he was younger. His student job as a funeral orator had furnished him with so many bizarre experiences that he had resorted to writing them down in a diary as a way of processing them. He couldn't remember what had possessed him to repackage the thing as a novel but, with the title *A Sad Affair*, he sent it off to a publisher, who to his surprise released it. Despite the novel's devastating commercial failure, Escher had remained a keen reader but had steadily moved away from literary novels in favor of Mafia books.

To calm himself he picked up the Mafia novel and looked for where he'd left off before being interrupted by the anonymous courier at the door. Marko Steiner spent the first night of his new life in Rome. Instead of enjoying his newfound freedom he fell into a deep sleep at the first station hotel he could find. His bones felt weighed down by all those virtually sleepless nights in prison. The fear of being shot did not subside until he'd locked and secured the door of his hotel room by wedging a chair beneath its old-fashioned handle. He'd even watched suspiciously as the hotel porter, for whom Marko Steiner was nothing more than someone in search of a bed for the night, photocopied his passport.

Right outside the window to his room shone the *L* of the HOTEL sign. When Marko Steiner awoke thirteen hours later, the *L* was no longer lit. He made his way to the station, where he drank a *doppio* and boarded the train to Milan. He was still feeling a little queasy because he'd stuffed himself the night before. He wondered why, of all the dishes he could have chosen, he'd picked the schnitzel. Maybe because of some extravagant desire to fit in with his future compatriots, or because he'd grown nostalgic for his prison stint since Sven had alternately referred to these very same compatriots as *schnitzel gobblers* and *schnitzel gobs*. It had taken him a long time to work out the difference. In his vocabulary book he'd also jotted down the exclamations that Sven often employed—"gobsmacked"—closely followed by "Shut your gob!" and "That gobshite!"

His own face was the reason that he'd scheduled a longer stop in Switzerland than would be necessary for visiting the bank. Although in Milan he missed his connection to Lugano, the next train got him there in time to withdraw the money from the bank and make an appointment with the surgeon.

The doctor gave him a curt greeting in strange-sounding Italian and was startled when Marko replied in German, "I'd like a new gob."

The doctor reacted to Marko's first words of German as a free man with a wanting frown that, while faintly articulated around his eyes, found little to no expression on his Botox-injected forehead. Marko wondered whether people in this part of Switzerland didn't like to hear German spoken aloud, or if it had just come down to his pronunciation. Meanwhile, the doctor forged ahead with his Italian as if Marko hadn't said anything and explained that the first appointment would be with his assistant. To Marko's surprise he wasn't going to be operated on immediately. This was just a consultation during which Marko could choose the shape of nose he wanted.

The doctor then disappeared into an operating room, leaving

Marko to browse a catalog of facial features with his assistant.

"Nose without a curve," Marko said, squeezing out the second German utterance of his new life.

The assistant smiled.

Then she continued in Italian. It sounded better than the surgeon's. She explained to Marko that it might not be a perfectly straight nose, as to achieve the best possible results you always had to work with the original shape.

"*Il suo naso ha una* big curve," the assistant giggled, indicating the model in the catalog his nose currently corresponded to. Then she explained that in his case a completely straight nose was out of the question.

"I don't give a shit."

Although—given his language tutor Sven's particular fondness for this turn of phrase—he was fairly confident he'd pronounced it correctly, the assistant gave a start.

"We'll make it as straight as we can."

He didn't have anything at all against a slight curve. In any case he'd have preferred to keep the boxer's nose he'd inherited from his father. His mother didn't have a straight nose either. Truthfully, Marko didn't trust perfectly straight noses. There was something haughty about them. You could forget women with straight noses, while men with straight noses were ridiculous. As the assistant leafed through the catalog, explaining the different shapes, he noticed her nose. She had a slightly too small, or more accurately, *flat* nose. As if it belonged to a different face. He suspected it wasn't an easy task to make a nose bigger. In this respect he was blessed, for all the noses in his family were proper ones that could easily be whittled down.

"If you're saying as straight a nose as possible, I'd go with model three," the assistant suggested, tapping with her gleaming red fingernail. "Although it's not perfectly straight, it would look more natural on your face than, say, model two."

"I want new eyebrows too," Marko demanded in Italian.

"That requires a separate appointment," the assistant informed him. "Eyebrows are a whole new ballgame."

"Not another appointment. *Now!*" protested Marko, who'd learned the art of negotiation from Luigi Mancuso.

"You'll have to take it up with the doctor."

Now that the assistant was on edge, her nose was beginning to suit her face, which had gone flat.

"Yes," Marko said, leaping to his feet. "I'll talk to him. Where is he?"

"He's operating right now."

"Good, I'll go and see him."

Horrified, the assistant talked him down. "Wait here, please. I'll fetch him."

She went into the treatment room and soon afterward the doctor came out and told Marko the same thing he'd just heard from his assistant. The doctor had quite a potato nose. Schnitzel gob with potato nose, Sven would have said. The surgeon explained to Marko that a nose job and browlift could not be done as a single procedure. He would not touch the eyebrows until the nose had properly healed.

Marko felt the blood rise to his head. In his previous life this conversation would have taken a very different course. If he were sitting here with the likes of Luigi Mancuso or Antonio Ranieri or Vittorio De Santis, the matter would have been quickly settled. Luigi would have grabbed the doctor by his scrawny neck and shoved his nose into the calendar until he could smell the operation date. *Nose and eyebrows, all in the next five minutes* would be pencilled in the calendar with his bloody nose. But Luigi Mancuso, Antonio Ranieri, and Vittorio De Santis were not here. They'd been pushing daisies since Palm Sunday two years ago.

"I'll pay cash," Marko countered.

"Cash or not," the doctor replied testily, "the browlift requires a separate appointment!"

Sweat gathered on the doctor's inflexible brow. He had seen this time and again, he explained to his irascible patient. People thought a browlift was a simple walk in the park compared to a nose job. This misconception arose from the nose's bombastic form and because a bone was involved. Not to mention if the surgeon's hand slipped, it wasn't far to the artery! These hard facts would always overshadow the underappreciated artistry of invisible stitches. In a natural arc. The eyebrows required something very different from the nose. German expressed it far better than Italian could. Did he know the term *Fingerspitzengefühl?*

This was not a word that Marko had ever heard fall from Sven's lips.

"*Fingerspitzengefühl.* It literally means 'fingertipsfeeling,' great sensitivity or instinct," the doctor said, pinching his fingers in a gesture that meant "Shut your gob!" where Marko came from. The doctor seemed to mean it in a very different way.

Reaching into his coat pocket, Marco retrieved the envelope with which he finally persuaded the doctor that his eyebrows did, in fact, require immediate attention. As the doctor counted the money, the tips of his fingers riffling the bills within the envelope, Marko repeated, "*Fingerspitzengefühl.*"

Instructing his assistant to dispatch another colleague into the operating room to wrap up the half-finished upper lip, the doctor ushered Marko into a second operating room. When he was asked to count down from one hundred, Marko had a go of it in German but didn't even make it to ninety-nine.

In the days following the operation Marko ventured out into the streets only at night. He wanted to wait until everything had properly healed. During the day he stayed in his hotel room, learning German and reading his book.

Before Escher made the call he went over to the dead man again. Like a child, he hoped the problem would solve itself. That the electrician would simply start being alive again. Then he kneeled beside the body and tried CPR once more. Now that it was too late, he made even more of an effort. After all, you could never be 100 percent sure. He didn't know what to hope for. If the electrician turned out not to be dead, he would have wasted all these valuable minutes and might be to blame for permanent damage.

But even after several minutes of chest compressions Escher

couldn't feel a pulse on the electrician's neck. He found it shameful that something as banal as a pulse could mean the difference between life and death. A mechanical indicator without any real substance. It was incomprehensible that you could wind up dead so quickly without noticing it. Escher was so angered by this that he embarked on another lifesaving attempt. He gave everything he had to bring the electrician back, battling for the life of this stiff puppet to the point of exhaustion. When he finally gave up, he lay sweating and snorting beside the body. He was so out of breath that he could not help but notice how dramatically his own chest was rising and falling. So, this was life. A rising and falling chest. Nothing of the sort was happening to the electrician.

Escher had never put much stock into the commonly held belief that a good death was one you weren't aware of. Maybe the electrician would have agreed with this popular take. At least he would have then lived out his preferred death. A nice one. A rapid one without torment and fear. Escher, on the other hand, had always considered this to be the most undignified of deaths. Imagine being unaware that your life was coming to an end. Not even having the time to pull all the threads together.

Ever since his first flight as an eighteen-year-old he'd been preoccupied with the question of where to channel his thoughts in the event of a plane crash. He wanted to be prepared so that he could quickly summon the right thought in an emergency. A thought that would rally him like a goal in the final seconds of a soccer match and preserve him from destruction. For this scenario, which he privately hoped would never come to pass, he wanted to have the appropriate thought process up his sleeve. Comforting thoughts. Conclusive thoughts. Interpretations of his own life that amounted to something. Loving memories of those close to him. Who were these people? And what exactly would you think of if you had only thirty seconds? Or maybe two to three minutes? You'd like to dedicate this time to worthy thoughts, not squander it on trivialities. A quick rundown of the good times and positive emotions, which undiluted, allowed your life to culminate with its very best moment: an interpretation of the life you'd lived that you'd be happy to let stand as a résumé.

This was without doubt a preferable death to the one that took you by surprise. And how much better it would be to take to heart these insights you'd saved up for a rainy day before it actually happened. Indeed, you could allow your normal, everyday life to be shaped by them. By issuing a lenient verdict on your existence and taking its lesson to heart, you could breeze through life even without plane crashes or illness.

In his novel *A Sad Affair*, published an eternity ago, he had put these deliberations to use in crafting the main character. This didn't impress the critics. One said that the protagonist was grappling with questions about the meaning of life that would be hard to stomach in a twelve-year-old's diary. Another had concluded, with relish, that although the laws of logic forbade self-referential statements, surely the sheer vacillation of this book warranted an exception: The novel was indeed "a sad affair."

When Escher's breathing had calmed again and his pulse more or less returned to normal, he rang the emergency services.

He knew it was futile, but he wanted everything to take its proper course as quickly as possible and for nobody to be able to level accusations at him. There was something aggressive about the curt questions he was asked on the phone; Escher merely replied with a "yes" to everything, and "yes" again, even declaring himself willing to continue with life-saving measures. To be on the safe side he didn't let slip that the electrician had been lying dead on the floor for half an hour already. Then Escher sat at the kitchen table and waited for the ambulance.

Despite the stentorian voice on the phone, which had signaled to Escher that there wasn't a second to be wasted, he found the time it took for the ambulance to arrive surprisingly long. For the second time that day he found himself waiting impatiently for the doorbell to ring. *Maybe from what I said they deduced it was too late*, he mused, *and they've prioritized other, more urgent cases*. Although he held out zero hope for the electrician, his anger grew with every minute of waiting. Was this what the country had come to, that the emergency services now made you wait? The tension he'd eased during his exhausting attempts at resuscitation returned. To avoid losing his head, he left the kitchen and went into the living room where he forced himself to read a few lines of his book.

Marko Steiner had made it through the operation. Having shed the protuberance of his typical Russo nose he had severed the connection to his people for good. The nose was straighter than he'd hoped. His new eyebrows lent him a faint air of surprise. As if he only now realized what he'd gotten himself into.

Or as if he'd been left permanently astonished by the fact that the Swiss bank had actually paid out his cash.

He wondered whether Falcone really knew nothing about this money or whether he had just been playing dumb. After all, they'd already given him money for the journey. Money from the state! Sometimes he wondered what they knew. Perhaps they'd simply turned a blind eye.

Up until the end he'd feared that they would grant him special protection as key witness only if he revealed the hideout of Gino, the boss of bosses. But they'd believed his story. That with his drone he'd smuggled the medication for Gino into prison, the medication that had allowed the boss to leave in a hearse. But that he didn't know where Franco Larini would be taking the hearse after he'd shot the driver. The only genuine corpse turned out to be the driver. The court was satisfied with Franco Larini's head. They didn't care about Elio's Swiss money. All they wanted was for him to snitch. For that they would fulfill all his wishes. But he had none apart from staying alive.

His savings were enough to get by for a year. Or three months if he stayed in Switzerland. That would have been the most comfortable arrangement. The people in this part of the country spoke Italian. Even though they had a ludicrous accent. But the judge had urged him to find a big city. Hamburg and Berlin were big. Cologne or Munich or Vienna were too. Hanover, Leipzig, and Dresden were also in the running.

He opted for Sven's hometown. An industrial city in the west of Germany. It was a shithole, Sven had told him, but still better than those other places. There was only one thing you had to know. Its name was Ü, which you pronounced by rounding the lips as if to say *oo* but saying *ee*. Sven, ever the strict teacher, had hammered this point home, pontificating in his junkie drawl.

"Ü!"

Everything in this *ü* gave his student lip spasms.

To reach Ü by train, after a four-hour journey he had to transfer at the border between Switzerland and Germany. He was pleased when nobody asked to see his passport. Although it wasn't a forgery, he put little trust in the document. There weren't any issues with transferring trains either. The Swiss train had arrived perfectly on time in Basel. Only four and a half hours till Ü. Seven hours later, Marko Steiner stepped off the German train in his new home city.

After spending a night in a hotel, he sublet a tiny apartment behind the station and started exploring the city. On his third day he found a flyer at a trolley stop that said, "German lessons for beginners and intermediates—taught by professional German teacher."

Falcone had warned him about language schools. They would be the first place anyone would come looking, if indeed someone was after him. Private tutoring, in this case administered by Frauke Schnabel, offered the perfect solution.

Marko didn't understand a single word that came out of the Nokia prepaid phone he'd bought at the station. The woman spoke a very different German from that of his junkie tutor.

"Slowly, please," he said. "My name is Marko Steiner and I need German."

"Oh, I'm very sorry. It's been a lifelong struggle. I speak too quickly."

She laughed like an opera singer. "Now I'm speaking very slowly," she said very slowly.

"Yes, thank you."

"Are you looking for lessons?"

"Yes, I need German."

"What is your mother tongue."

"German," he said.

"You already speak a bit of German?"

"Yes, not much. I have a German friend. I can understand. I can read. But chattin' ain't so good."

"Chattin' ain't so good!" the woman laughed.

"Yes."

"Where are you now?"

"I don't know exactly."

"Come to Café Schirm."

"Yes—I don't give a shit."

"Will you find it?"

"Obvs."

"Café Schirm in Mercatorstrasse. Not far from McDonald's," she added, just to be sure. "You're bound to find it."

"Obvs."

"Two p.m.?"

"Okey-doke."

"Two p.m. today?"

"Yes, okey-doke."

Frauke Schnabel arrived outside Café Schirm at two p.m. on the dot. She was as old as his grandmother and as thin as Donatella who, it was said, didn't eat for a year after the heads of both her sons were discovered in the hairdresser's window display. What singled her out from those two women, however, were her broad horse's smile, dyed-blond hair, and strikingly tacky getup.

"Are you Marko?" she asked in a crazed pitch.

"Yes, Marko Steiner," Marko said, offering his hand.

"I'm Frauke," she said, shaking his hand with a laugh.

She had all her teeth. No gold ones.

"You didn't need to wait outside for me in this heat."

Her eyes were an unnatural blue. Like the marbles they used to play with as children. You'd make a little divot in the earth with a scrape of your heel. Then you'd stand five yards away and try to roll your *biglia* into the hole. Whoever managed it first won the others' marbles. When someone had won all the marbles, they were promptly beaten up. Frauke held open the door to the café for him.

"It's nice in here," Frauke observed, very loudly. "What would you like to drink?"

"Tea," Marko said, because although he craved an espresso, he didn't want his pronunciation to give him away. Dreaming of this first espresso in freedom, he resigned himself to the fact that there was no way he could squeeze the word from his throat as crudely as Sven had done.

Frauke frowned at the menu. "They've got peppermint tea,

good form tea, mountain herb mixture, jasmine, rooibos tea, Earl Grey, Ceylon."

"I'll have the good vorm tea."

Frauke laughed. "One good vorm tea," she said to the waiter, who kept a straight face.

"And a white coffee for me, please."

"Do you understand 'good form tea'?"

"Obvs. Good tea, vorm. Not too cold, not too hot."

"The word is 'form,' not 'warm' or 'vorm,' as you pronounced it."

"Form," Marko repeated.

"It's how you feel. If you feel good, you're in good form. Drinking the tea makes you feel good. Supposedly!"

"Good form, my ass," Marko said. "That doesn't come from the tea."

"How do you know these expressions?" Frauke chortled. "They make me feel in really good form!"

When the waiter brought their drinks, Frauke said. "Careful, it's hot, not warm." She laughed at her own joke.

Marko lowered the teabag into the cup and said, "What do I have to shell out for this?"

"It's on me, my treat."

"I mean, for the lesson."

Frauke laughed out loud. "That's very good!"

She was amused by her mistake. "I'm afraid I can't treat you to the lessons. How would I live?"

"You're in good form," Marko said.

"Yes, always. I'm always in good form."

"Because the tea?"

"No, not because *of* the tea," Frauke said, emphasizing the correction, as if meaning to etch it into her new pupil's mind. "How often would you like to have lessons?"

"Three hours," Marko said, thrusting three fingers into the air.

"Three hours per week," Frauke nodded. "That's good, I think—"

"Three hours every day," Marko said.

Frauke looked shocked. Marko was unfazed.

"Are you being serious?"

"You bet your ass I am!"

Frauke laughed and shook her head, which did not put him in good form. All the same, they met again the following day, spending three hours at Café Schirm. And the day after. And every day after that. Even when he was not with Frauke, Marko was learning German.

While he was making good headway in the book Sven had given him, there were still sentences that stumped him. Whenever this happened, he brought the book along to his lesson and asked Frauke for help.

"What's that you're reading?" she asked with a frown.

He opened the book and pointed to the passage.

Frauke read the line and shook her head. "That's dialect."

She read it again.

"I'm not totally sure. Let me read the section from the beginning. Maybe I'll get it from the context."

A song tore Escher from his reading. Again, it was the electrician's cell, so loud it seemed as if it were the last attempt to raise him from the dead. The endless repetition of the tune every three seconds got on Escher's nerves. He was nauseated by all those scraps of music that were blasted into your ears in public. It was worst of all in the trolley or on the subway, where there was no escape. Once, on a long train journey, his entire car had been driven up the wall by a phone buried in some unknown passenger's luggage. At least the electrician's cell wasn't making the usual techno rattle. On the contrary, it was a song by Escher's favorite singer.

"*Wa ye callin' ma on ma fone?*" the heartbroken man begged an ex.

Escher didn't know whether to laugh or cry at the ringtone's plea. There was something rather indecent about laughing over the dead man he'd been trying to revive only a few minutes ago. *Really original, this choice of ringtone*, Escher couldn't help thinking. And there was no letup from the singer, who lamented over and over again, "*Why ye callin' ma on ma fone? Surely ye ken where t'find ma home.*" At this point the recording cut the singer off mid-sentence, catapulting him back to the beginning: "*Why ye callin' ma on ma fone? Surely ye ken where t'find—*"

"*Ma home*," Escher's brain couldn't help finishing, while the refrain began anew.

He'd have loved to have been able to congratulate the dead man on his excellent choice of ringtone. He wouldn't have credited this taciturn type with such a sharp sense of humor. Even for someone alive, "*Why ye callin' ma on ma fone?*" was a sassy challenge to any caller that was hard to trump. But from a dead man there was something hair-raising about the bitter sarcasm. And yet again the singer bewailed, "*Why ye callin' ma on ma fone? Surely ye ken where t'find—*"

"*Ma home*," Escher's brain finished the line again as the loop restarted for the umpteenth time, breaking off at the same place and subconsciously prompting Escher to complete it. With every repetition he became more painfully aware that the electrician wouldn't be going back home ever again. Escher waited for the voicemail to kick in, but the electrician must have disabled it, affording no end to the repetition.

Most likely someone from the firm was trying to get ahold of their colleague, maybe the boss of Elektro Janko whom Escher had called originally, wanting to know how the job was going. Presumably the electrician ought to have finished by now and arrived at his next job. Eventually the caller's patience ran out and the phone fell silent.

But the peace lasted only for a few seconds.

"*Why ye callin' ma on ma fone? Surely ye ken where t'find—*" cranked up again.

"*Ma home.*" Escher must put a stop to this brainwashing. The simplest thing would be to take the call. But he didn't want to fish a cell out from the dead man's pocket. It couldn't be long before the ambulance finally showed, and then everything would take its own course anyway.

"*Why ye callin' ma on ma fone? Surely ye ken where t'find—*"

"*Ma home.*" Putting the phone on silent didn't seem like a sensible idea either. His fingerprints on the dead man's device could get him into trouble. On the whole, it was better to leave everything as it was. The emergency doctor would know what to do. Maybe they'd notify the police and the police could inform the employer. The thought of the police made Escher uneasy. As did the idea of a doctor turning up needlessly or an overwhelmed boss pacing up and down his apartment in a sweat. At least the music had stopped, thank God. This prevented him from losing it altogether, though the phone might start up again at any time.

To prevent the wait from stretching out into eternity, he forced himself to go back to his book until the ambulance arrived. But Escher found it almost impossible to concentrate. He was on permanent alert. The police might turn up any second now. But his mind was also spinning as he thought about the potential consequences this death held for his life. He knew that what he'd done wasn't murder. At worst it was involuntary manslaughter. It was only murder if you killed someone with intent. But there was no question of a deliberate killing here. Even the bit about negligence was debatable. Didn't negligence admit a willingness to take risks? Like the speeding driver who consciously drives over the limit even though they have no intention of killing any-one. But what Escher had done was in error, closer to an accident than an act of negligence. Simply bad luck! More comparable to a stumble that plunges another person into the abyss. Escher's mind was still preoccupied by these thoughts as he read the first few lines, but eventually he managed to lose himself in the book.

Marko Steiner's head felt so heavy from learning his new mother tongue (and forgetting his old one) that he bought himself some running shoes and began to go jogging for hours. This naturally brought him into contact with more people, and the language practiced itself. Not only could he silently name the things he passed, comment on them, and situate them in the future and the past, he could also hurl new insults at drivers who cut him off. Do you need glasses? Sleepyhead! Dreamer! Frauke's insults weren't up to snuff. It was hard to improve on curses from childhood with these new ones. Fortunately, he still had some of Sven's expressions up his sleeve. Sven's vocabulary earned him respect from the fuckwits and douchebags who drove like retards.

Having said that, Marko himself was responsible for most of the collisions. He didn't pay attention to traffic. When out jogging he would let the conjugations run through his mind. He traveled through the tenses. I run, I ran, I will run. I had run, the sweat ran. I run, you run, it runs. I turn. The traffic light turns. The traffic light turned. To red. I will cross the road, although. Although the traffic light turned to red. There will not have been a cop in sight.

"You don't need that," Frauke explained. "That's the future perfect, nobody can do that. You can skip the future perfect and the pluperfect."

For the most part Frauke was a strict teacher, but she didn't want the future perfect. What she was really allergic to, however, was the German he'd learned from his drug dealer.

"That's dreadful slang," Frauke kept saying. "Who taught you that?"

"It's how young people in Switzerland talk."

Frauke gave a resounding laugh. "That's how young people in Switzerland talk? More likely young people in the slammer."

Marko Steiner grinned. "You don't say 'the slammer.' You say 'penal institution.'"

"'Prison' will do," Frauke said. "And you don't have to say 'hooch'; you can also say 'alcohol.'"

"I don't drink alcohol anyway. It gives you a tongue like a badger's asshole."

"A dry mouth," Frauke corrected him, horrified.

"Yes," Marko Steiner. "Both are correct."

"What do you mean, 'Both are correct'?"

"Alcohol gives you a dry mouth. Hooch gives you a tongue like a badger's asshole. Makes you stink like fuck."

Frauke had guessed early on, of course, that he hadn't learned his German at an elite Swiss boarding school. But she didn't probe. Marko Steiner was pleased by her discretion. And she didn't react with disappointment when he asked to meet only twice a week.

"Soon you'll be raring to go," Frauke said.

"Raring to go?"

When Frauke explained this term to him, Marko felt as if she'd seen right through him. He had in fact just bought an old bicycle that someone had been advertising by the roadside with a cardboard sign.

"Broken, but fixable. Fifty D-marks."

Although the country had just switched to a new currency,

Marko thought it most fitting that an old bike should be offered in the old one. He contacted the seller, who, to his surprise, was younger than the bicycle and knocked down the price by twenty marks. Anyone who can negotiate a bike down from fifty to thirty marks in a new language is soon going to be raring to go. When repairing the bike, Marko made sure that he could fix a word to every part and a phrase to every action. After a few days his lexicon was greasier than the chain. I grease the chain. I dismantle the gears. I derust the cogwheels. Who rests, rusts. I roast, I got roasted. After he had rested, he raced off. I renew the wiring. I put every spoke back in. The spoke, the spike. The spark. The spoke rusts, the spike raps, the spark rips. A spoke is broken and needs to be replaced. The spoke, the rim. Speak, spoke, spoken. The rim, the rhyme. The ball bearing. The cog. The frog.

When the bike was ready he covered the city in a day. Forty-five miles. I cycle. I pedal. It is beautiful to circle the city. To ride through the forest. To traverse the fields. Motorways drone. Fallow land blooms. Rivers run. Slag heaps abound. Rowing clubs are beside the towpath. Mission. Permission. Permitted thoroughfare. Until revoked.

Every day he rode farther, discovering new words everywhere. His calves grew large, as if they were storing words. One day his bike was gone. I steal, I stole. I stole away.

He'd stolen away without having locked up the bike. Piss, pee, piddle, answer the call of nature, pop to the loo. He leaned the bike against a tree, against the bark (bike, bark, book, break) and went into the woods. When he came back the bike was gone.

He could see the thief in the distance. Running after him, he cried, "That's my bike! I'm going to kill you, you wanker!"

It was good thing that Frauke hadn't heard him. Another woman came past and looked at him sympathetically. "Did he nick your bike?"

"Yes," Marko said. "Nicked, stolen. Pilfered. I just needed to go and then the bike was gone."

"Oh, you poor thing," the woman said with her extra- (*He'd noticed that when there was something Frauke particularly liked she didn't just use the word* extraordinary *but split it in two. Observing a pause in which the extraordinariness could unfold. Now he understood why she did this.*) -ordinarily beautiful mouth. This woman with her extraordinarily beautiful teeth had a smile one ought to require a permit for.

What her mouth said was: "Bicycle theft is getting worse and worse. Shall I call the cops?"

But her eyes were saying to the sporty cyclist with the almost straight nose and surprised eyebrows, "You're just my cup of tea."

"No!" he replied in horror. "No need for cops. It was an old bike."

Triggered by her offer to call the police, he spewed out more sentences than ever: "The value was low. I acquired it in a defective state. It didn't cost much. It was a bargain. But it took me a lot of time to repair. Derusting the cogwheels was a pain. Adjusting the gears was tricky. Wiring the gear shift was a tedious procedure. The brake pads and cables needed replacing. I put in two new spokes to prevent the rim from sagging."

She looked at him with such astonishment, as if a talking robot had emerged from the woods.

"What are you going to do now without a bicycle? I mean, this is the asscrack of the world," the woman said to the strange man whose handsome head was coming up with these laborious sentences.

"The asscrack of the world," Marko repeated, thinking of Sven, from whom he'd picked up this lovely phrase. "Maybe I'll take the bus."

"There are no buses here," she said, offering him a lift. Her car was nearby.

A few hours later she told him, "You got caught in my web. I abducted you."

"Abducted," Marko laughed, allowing the word to melt in his mouth. "Abducted. That cracks me up."

"It's no laughing matter. You're just my cup of tea. Do you know who you remind me of?"

Remind, reminding, reminded, Marko thought without replying.

"A guy I once met on vacation," she said. "It was in the very south of Italy. In Aspromonte. Have you ever been there? It's extra—"

Marko hoped she wouldn't say any more.

"—ordinarily beautiful. You could be from there, you really could. The guy, his name was Rino—wow, I didn't think I'd remember the name."

Marko was suddenly in an extra-ordinary rush to get out of her apartment. He took two things from the experience. A new idiom and an important realization. *Human contact is not my cup of tea*, Marko accepted, and holed up at home for a few days. His cup of tea was new words and new sentences. As well as the book that Sven had given him, which he took out again. By now he was able to read it almost fluently.

Escher's own phone was ringing in unison with the electrician's. When he finally took the call he discovered that the emergency services had been waiting outside his door for ten minutes. If he didn't let them in right away, they warned, he might be fined.

"I didn't hear anything!"

"Did you switch off the doorbell?"

"Of course not. But our bell is always on the fritz," he claimed, first pressing the white button to reactivate the doorbell, then the blue one to open the door.

Seconds later Escher's apartment was populated by four strangers (not including the dead man). A red-haired ambulance driver, a peeved emergency doctor, Herr Janko from the firm Elektro Janko, and the police officer Janko had rung when Escher didn't open the door.

It didn't take long for the doctor to declare the electrician dead, and so she spent most of her time typing everything up on her tablet. She asked Herr Janko to enter the details of his employee himself. He had to ring the office to get the social security number and date of birth. Janko was the youngest person there, which confused Escher. Was he only the junior boss? Did his father not think the death of an employee important enough to attend to the matter himself? Or had the father himself died young, misfortune forcing a premature succession on the family? These sorts of things were not so easy to suss out. The boss (or junior boss) was beside himself and yet he strove to assure the police officer that there had been no negligence on the part of the firm.

"He was an experienced man," he declared indignantly. "This sort of thing doesn't happen to a pro like him. He's been an excellent colleague for years. A reliable man."

Escher was cross that this insolent brat was calling the experienced corpse "reliable."

"He's trained apprentices," young Janko said. "I actually did my apprenticeship with him. My father thought the world of him."

"Is your father no longer part of the firm?" the policeman asked.

"My father died unexpectedly a year ago."

Escher cleared his throat awkwardly. As if he, rather than the policeman, had asked the question about Janko's father. Even more embarrassing than his curiosity was the fact that his assumption had been right. All the same, he wondered whether the phrase "died unexpectedly" was a euphemism for suicide. It had struck him when reading the papers that, when it came to death, the two main types of announcements were "after a long and serious illness" and "died unexpectedly." Long and serious illness meant cancer; died unexpectedly meant suicide. It was never spelled out, to prevent putting any ideas into people's heads—

nobody wanted copycat suicides. This was the media acting responsibly. They overdid it, however, and after the article would include something along the lines of, "If you suffer from depression or suicidal thoughts, please ring the following number." Such well-intentioned advice undermined the earlier discretion. Escher wondered whether there were two different departments at work here: one responsible for discretion in the article, the other for the suicide-prevention PSA. Or if there was a dilemma behind it. The editor had realized that potential suicide victims knew full well what was meant by "died unexpectedly" because they soaked up pertinent information. And thus it was not so bad that the PSA canceled out the taboo in the article.

If a reference to the advice hotline was missing, you could assume that "died unexpectedly" referred to a stroke or a heart attack. You could rule out an accident because in such cases the piece usually said "accident." For the first time Escher now wondered how the electrician's death would be reported in the news. Under digest. An electrician suffered a fatal accident while working in a private apartment. The cause of the accident—"*Why ye callin' ma on ma fone? Surely ye ken where t'find—*"

The singer was interrupted by the young boss, who had stepped smartly over to the body and removed the cell from the dungarees.

"Can you believe he's dead?" he cried into the phone.

The distraught tinny voice that rang out was immediately interrupted again: "No, I've got no idea either! I haven't a clue. He didn't switch off the breakers! But what do I know?"

He listened for a second or two, then said, "Look, I've got to go, the police are here. I'll call you back soon."

"You shouldn't have touched that phone before everything here was cataloged." Escher was taken aback that these words came not from the policeman but from the young ambulance driver.

"What?" the incensed young boss said.

"You shouldn't touch anything until everything is clear."

"Right, I suppose there'll be an investigation now, won't there?" Janko asked, unnerved, staring blankly at the telephone in his hands.

Escher watched his face, which had already gone red during the telephone call, now assume a darker shade. The driver's hair was red too, but these were such completely different colors that Escher wondered how the same word could be used to describe them both.

The police officer shrugged. He didn't seem to know with any certainty what would happen in a case like this.

"We'll have to take a look first," he said in a downbeat voice. "Don't touch anything else."

As if he had to save face after the overzealous driver's comment, the policeman turned to Escher. He fixed him with an emphatic stare and asked about the course of events.

"Did you notice that the electrician had forgotten to flip the circuit breakers?"

"I wasn't paying any attention."

"Maybe he interrupted his work and switched them back on again?" the officer now suggested.

"No," Escher said. "He'd only just gotten started. Why would he interrupt his work?"

"Maybe he was testing something? Or he had to go and fetch something?"

"No, he didn't fetch anything."

The young boss accompanied each of the policeman's questions with an irritated shake of the head, as if he were about to interrupt. But he said nothing.

"Where exactly were you standing?" the policeman asked. "Did you witness the accident?"

"I was in the living room. Reading," Escher said.

"You were reading while the electrician was working?"

Escher felt like asking the officer if that was illegal. But he was on his guard and was not going to allow himself to be provoked.

"Yes, I didn't want to disturb him. I mean, I hate it when someone's looking over my shoulder when I'm working."

"What then?"

"There was a sudden thud. As if he'd fallen off the ladder. But he wasn't standing on a ladder. That's what it sounded like, though—he hit the floor noisily."

"Did you see that?"

"No, I didn't see it. I heard it! First I heard it, then of course I came hurrying in and saw him lying there."

"What were you reading?"

"I'm sorry?"

Escher wondered whether this was a particularly sophisticated interrogation technique. Why was the police officer interested in the book? Did he doubt Escher's version of events? Was he trying to get him to contradict himself? Did he think that Escher had accidentally flipped the circuit breakers back on? Unconsciously. Without thinking about it.

"I want to know what you were reading," the policeman said again.

"This book," Escher said, picking it up off the table and showing it to the officer.

"Oh, that one. I know it, I've read it too."

"Really?"

"Yes, about the mafiosi in the witness-protection program."

Escher would have preferred him to have said *mafioso*, but he didn't let on.

"It's a fantastic book," the policeman said.

"Yes, it is."

"What part have you got to?"

Escher became suspicious once more. What was the policeman up to? Was he trying to trip him up?

"Where he goes from Milan to Switzerland," Escher lied.

He had absolutely no idea why he had done so.

"Actually, you don't say 'Mafia,'" the driver butted in again. "You say ''Ndrangheta' or 'Camorra' or 'Cosa Nostra.' Depending on where. One's in Sicily, the others are more on the mainland."

Luckily, at that very moment the emergency doctor was called to her next case, and the impertinent driver left with her.

"Yes, that's a great bit," the officer said. "Where he's on the train and addressed by his new name for the first time. 'Are you Herr Marko Steiner?' But it gets better. When he arrives in

Germany, wanders around, and everything seems completely alien. But I don't want to give away too much."

"It must be brutal in witness protection."

"We get some of them occasionally. Starting completely from scratch again isn't easy at all."

Janko listened, disconcerted, and when Escher said no more about the book, an uncomfortable silence ensued. An angel passed through the room. Escher loved this expression. Unlike Raphael's angels, which he had as a puzzle but couldn't stand. Escher thought they looked like idiots rather than angels.

"So, what now?" Escher asked the policeman. "I don't want to sound heartless. But, to be honest, I'd rather not have a dead body lying around here forever."

"I don't think much more is going to happen," the police officer said. "It's a cut-and-dried case. Work accident. But we have to do everything by the book. Because of the insurance. So the widow gets her money."

"Widow?"

"Yes, the wife. Didn't you notice the wedding ring?"

"Oh yes, I did," Escher said. "It's just that everything's happened so quickly."

He didn't want to have to tell the policeman that it was the word *widow* that bothered him.

"It's such a shame, such a young man," the policeman said.

"How old is he?" Escher asked.

He hoped that nobody would correct this to *was*. Didn't the dead man have an age? Maybe he had an age for a few more days and then that was it—after that his whole life was of equal importance and the sequence of years and days no longer played any role.

"Mid-forties," Janko said.

"Children?"

"A young daughter, so far as I know."

"Has the wife been told?" Escher asked.

"*Why ye callin' me on ma fone? Ye ken where t'find—*"

"*Ma home*," Escher's brain added.

Nobody touched the phone and it stopped ringing in the middle of the third loop.

When the body was finally taken away, Escher was surprised that Janko and the policeman did not leave his apartment along with the stretcher. But they did go a minute or so later, as if their only reason for the delay was to maintain a certain distance. As he stood at the door Escher saw that the dead man's shoes were still there. He offered the shoes to the young boss, who took them silently.

The empty apartment seemed smaller now than when it had been full of people. The angel had left too. Escher opened all the windows and cleaned the floor where the electrician's body had lain. He was in need of some fresh air too. He just wanted to stretch out for a bit on the sofa first but fell asleep at once. Ten minutes later a phone call woke him from his deep sleep. The policeman asked him if he'd left his sunglasses in the apartment.

"I think I left them on your kitchen table."

Escher went to check.

"No, they're not there. I don't see them anywhere else, either. Sorry."

He wondered whether the officer really had mislaid his sunglasses or whether it was a ruse. He felt dizzy from having leaped up too quickly and so he lay back down on the sofa. A few more pages of his book was just the right thing to slowly get him back into gear. He was annoyed that he'd shut the book while being questioned by the policeman. Not having the patience to search for the right place, he took his chances at where the book opened.

Marko Steiner had found a new career more quickly than he'd expected. Restoring old bikes, at first for personal use, then as a paid hobby, had developed into a simple living. Business improved from week to week. Soon he wasn't just repairing his customers' bikes, but buying wrecks from flea markets and garage sales, salvaging their usable parts to create gorgeous new racers, and then selling them. His customers included pensioners, students, businesspeople, and even a vicar.

As word-of-mouth grew an ever-expanding customer base for him, he opened a proper workshop with a sales counter attached and had his business registered under the name RAREST. His pricey restored racers soon became trendy among fans of vintage cycles, and his discreet RAREST workshop sticker placed next to the famous Peugeot, Mercier, or KOGA logos enhanced the prestige of the original brand. For aficionados, it was a point of pride to know the origin of the brand name. RAREST: RAcer REpair STeiner.

In the first few years, however, there was a sour note for the

RAREST fans. Friendly Herr Steiner refused point blank to repair Italian models. No Bianchi made its way into his workshop, let alone a Masi, GIOS, or De Rosa. The spurned lovers of beautiful Pinarellos could not suspect that this insistence pained Marko Steiner more than anyone. But he hadn't forgotten Falcone's warnings and wished to avoid the temptation of ordering spare parts from Italy. In his old language. Anyone who started down that path would sooner or later head to where they thought they might pick up old bike frames.

A Pinarello was the reason that, even as a child, Marko Steiner had become a master mechanic for racers. After Aldo Pisi died in the shootout in the church of Santa Maria, his widow sent the ten-year-old Elio her husband's bike. It was a gleaming treasure. A sacred object. The Campagnolo Super Record gear mechanism and the Cinelli handlebars that normally meant so much to him counted for little in this instance. For the steel frame of Aldo Pisi's Pinarello was clad in twenty-four-carat gold and shone like the priest's monstrance.

When he eventually lifted the ban on Italian brands it had nothing to do with the fact that on August 17, 2007, in the fifth year of his new life and four years since the official opening of RAREST, his photo appeared on German television. As every evening, he finished his working day by watching the TV news. To begin with, he'd taken the way the doom-laden faces of the German presenters glared at him personally, as if he'd committed a crime. Now, however, there really was something to be worried about. They were looking for him in connection with a sextuple murder that had taken place in Ü on August 15. His own eyes were now staring back at him from the television screen.

Marko Steiner forced himself to remain calm and avoid doing anything rash. Fortunately, he was wearing his motorcycle helmet in the photograph and only his eyes were visible. Don't lose your nerve. Keep a clear head. Be as cool as a cucumber. Don't let it get to you. Don't be fazed. Pull yourself together. Keep your composure. Don't jump the gun. He put his "On Vacation" sign on the RAREST door and went to his loft bed behind the workshop. He mustn't be seen in public over the next few days. He had to wait. To stop himself from going mad, he picked up his book and started reading where he'd left off a few days earlier.

No sooner had the policeman called about his sunglasses than Escher's cell phone rang again. Frau Janko was on the phone. Escher wondered whether this was the young boss's wife or his mother. Or his sister?

She apologized for the inconvenience that the accident had caused.

"We could send another electrician today, to finish the job."

Escher hadn't been expecting this, even though he rarely found himself surprised. As a very young boy he'd gotten used to forestalling potential surprises. Through anticipation. You always had to be a step ahead of what was going on, like a careful driver who predicts the truck swinging out in front of him. You had to be prepared. He even found the expressions of surprised people disagreeable. The unsuspecting fools looked like real Muppets.

The offer to have the outlet repaired that day, however, did take Escher by complete surprise. He was glad that Frau Janko couldn't see him. His voice didn't give anything away, and the hesitation in his response was probably imperceptible. Besides, Frau Janko was anything but suspicious. She didn't once question Escher's version of events. On the contrary, she apologized to him. She emphasized that the firm wasn't now going to make him wait for the repair as well.

"Or if today's a bit soon for you," she said, "we could wait for you to ring us as soon as—"

"It's not important," he interrupted her.

"Sure. But it can't be left as it is."

He wanted to ask how the dead man's wife was. The widow. But the question was so preposterous that instead he asked, "Has the wife been told?"

"Yes."

"By you?"

"Yes."

He wondered whether Frau Janko had telephoned or driven to see the woman. He was also curious to know the exact words she used to break the news to the widow. While he weighed which question wouldn't be too indiscreet and just about acceptable, he detected a change in Frau Janko's silence. Although he couldn't hear anything, he fancied he could sense her secretly weeping.

"That's fate," he said to fill the silence and give her time to get her crying under control.

"It's terrible," she said after a pause. "Our firm's been in existence for forty-three years. But nothing like this has ever happened before. An experienced electrician doesn't forget to switch off the breakers."

"Is someone looking after his wife? Where is she now?"

"A friend is with her."

"Any children?"

"A daughter. Thirteen or fourteen. She doesn't know yet. I think she'd had some sort of argument with her dad. Maybe that's why he wasn't . . . why he wasn't quite on the ball. So, would you like me to send someone round now?"

"I'd rather you check with the police first whether it's alright to change anything."

"I've already done that. It's not a problem, we can finish the job. They've photographed everything. Besides, what could there be of interest to them?"

"Not today," Escher said. "I'm too tired. I don't know why, but I'm really tired."

"I'm tired too. It's the shock. Worked up and tired at the same time. I'm so nervous and yet so exhausted too."

Escher wondered how this tiredness arose in someone's head. It was as if the energy of the electric shock had not only brought the organism of the electrician to a complete stop, but also had worn out those standing nearby.

"How many do you have on staff?"

"Why do you ask?"

"Well, I mean, you've got one fewer now. Perhaps it isn't so easy for you to assign another one to me."

She gave a curt laugh. A laugh of resignation, as if she could no longer imagine a world in which something so minor could count as a worry.

"We've got a staff of nine. A secretary, six electricians, and two apprentices. Well, five electricians now."

"Maybe we should wait until the funeral's over."

It struck Escher as disrespectful if another person finished the dead electrician's work before he was buried. Of course it didn't hurt the dead man any longer. But it might hurt the living man who this dead man had once been. And it hurt the dead man who Escher would be one day. It was hard to pinpoint from where in time such pain originated (future perfect? pluperfect?) and how to be rid of it.

"What's it got to do with the funeral?"

"Nothing, of course. All I'm saying is that I bet you've got a lot to do right now. Doesn't this sort of thing involve a huge amount of paperwork?"

"It hadn't crossed my mind. First up, I've got to look for a new electrician. We needed another one anyway. An extra one! But now I've got to find a replacement first. Oh well, I don't want to go on moaning to you. I feel really sorry for the wife. The widow."

"Nobody likes saying 'widow.'"

"No."

It felt to Escher as if the electrician hadn't properly died until now. When his wife was described as a widow.

"Is there anything that can be done for her? For the wife?"

"We're doing a collection."

"Can I contribute?"

"You don't have to and nor should you. You've been through enough. We'll sort it out. But, if you really want to pop something in the envelope, then sure. The more we collect, the better. It can't be any comfort, but at least it's a little bit of help."

Escher pondered what would be an appropriate donation. He was keen to help the widow. But it mustn't be so much that it looked like an admission of guilt.

"May I ask what sort of amount one gives?"

"No idea. I need to talk to my husband about it."

"I'll come round today and put something in the envelope. How long will you be there?"

"Tomorrow would be better," she said wearily. "My nerves are shot."

"Yes, tomorrow. How old was he?"

"How old?"

"Yes."

"Not quite forty-three."

"That's no age."

"No. If you come tomorrow we can also schedule another appointment."

Escher said goodbye, sat on the sofa, and for a while thought about how much he should put in the envelope. It probably wasn't an envelope but a small, flat cardboard box that you could discreetly slip money into without Frau Janko seeing. He hoped at the very least that it wouldn't be one of those unseemly tip jars that you increasingly saw on sales counters, or—God forbid!—a piggy bank.

One possibility might be to publicly donate an unremarkable

sum and secretly leave an anonymous donation for the wife. For the widow. The word *widow* sounded alien and archaic. He didn't know any widows personally. Apart, perhaps, from widows who were so ancient that you no longer regarded them as widows, merely old women who lived alone and whose husbands were long forgotten. Curious to know where this strange word came from, he Googled it.

"The designation *widowed* is, besides *single, married,* and *divorced,* one of the four types of family status."

This statement angered Escher. He had never seen himself as *single*. Rather, he felt unaffected by the question of family status, because he'd never made a decision in this regard. After all, a pedestrian wasn't a "carless person."

He found it interesting that *widower* was the derivative of *widow*. The article claimed that this was one of the few masculine terms derived from the feminine form.

Escher pondered what this meant, but all he could find was an etymological explanation for the word's origin.

"The word 'widow' goes back to the Indo-Germanic verbal root 'uidh'—be empty, lack."

Escher allowed the sound to melt in his mouth: *uidh*. It felt good. Like a mantra that irresistibly cozies up to you.

Uidh.

Be empty.

Uidh.

It sounded like an exquisite flavor: an ice-cream flavor. Or a healing balm. *Uidh.* The emptiness reminded him that he needed to go back and read the pages he'd skipped in his book.

The Mafia village was haunted by widows. The black phantoms had come to represent unmistakable breaks in the chain, grim tokens by which you could tally the murders in the village. Over the centuries a blood feud between rival families had produced an eerie surfeit of these ghosts. Murders committed as retribution for murders committed as retribution. And the more men who were violently dispatched, the more widows doting on orphaned sons, who in turn grew up to be brutal killers who produced more widows.

It was one of these widows who'd given ten-year-old Elio the golden Pinarello racer of her dead husband Aldo. Four years after its opening, RAREST finally lifted the ban on Italian racers. The boycott had led to too many questions. Besides, Marko felt that such caution five years after the start of his new life was excessive.

Soon he bought his first Pinarello wreck to fix up and sell. This was followed by a second. People were practically grabbing the bikes out of his hands. And because it wasn't easy to get hold of good Pinarellos in Germany, he began ordering them from Italy. He didn't actually go there, of course, but ordered them online. He paid with his credit card, which, naturally, was in the name of Marko Steiner. These orders didn't give him away. His photograph hadn't appeared on television because of his booming trade in Pinarellos. He didn't go there. Not to Italy. Italy only began south of Naples. And he didn't even go to Rome. Not even to Milan. It had never been a problem.

Nor was his crucial mistake the fact that he'd responded to an ad from a widow whose husband had willed her three garages full of rubbish. That was all a part of doing business. The old woman didn't seem particularly troubled by her husband's death. Finally, she could sell his junk that not only exceeded three garages but also rambled across half the garden. The hoarder had left her a mountain of old television sets, kitchen appliances, toys, all manner of spare parts, and several tons of rotting books. This hell seemed to contain the entire world of conceivable things and words. Loungers, coffee tables, hair dryers, shades, lampshades, sunshades, cameras, light bulbs, cathode-ray tube televisions, suitcases, radios, drills. Many of these things, still in their original packaging, would fetch a good price.

Marko bought the frames of two Pinarellos off her and several boxes of spare parts. None of this could be described as the mistake. He left the Panini album of the 1986 Italian football team, even though it was only missing pictures of Altobelli and the coach Bearzot. It was only when he got to the third garage that Marko stumbled across the Vespa hidden beneath a plastic tarpaulin. It wasn't in good condition, but everything was original and nobody had tinkered about with it. Of course he didn't restore Vespas. Not for customers. He wouldn't have gone that far. But it was a 1968 Primavera. The model his grandfather had ridden.

"Are you interested?" the widow asked.

Marko Steiner shook his head.

"Can't you use it?"

The Vespa had never started again after his grandfather's death. Venerated like the relic of the Madonna's hair in the town of All Graces, it lay at rest in the garage. Elio had hoped to get the Primavera at some point, until the day the garage went up in flames.

"Actually, on second thought, yes," Marko said. "I'll take it."

Buying the Vespa wasn't necessarily the crucial mistake. After all, he had no intention of selling it, ever. He wasn't even interested in riding it himself. He just wanted to give it a new lease on life. The Primavera should end up as good as new.

It was only when he hid it from himself in the workshop, tucking it into the farthest corner of the basement's storage space, that it began to feel like a mistake. Before he could begin dismantling it, he had to shake off this feeling. You must never start restoring something in a moment when you're not at your best. It was fortunate that, in clearing out the storage space for the Vespa, he came across Sven's book. He'd never finished it. He looked for the place where he'd stopped reading.

Escher suppressed the urge to head straight to the Elektro Janko office and add his contribution to the collection. It would have made him feel better, but it seemed disrespectful to fork over money to the widow so hastily. It would be improper to immediately respond to the tragedy with a financial donation. False comfort for the widow. *Uidh.* The emptiness warranted a certain amount of time. The absence must be afforded space.

From his research into funeral rituals he understood how different cultures dealt with loss. He knew there were cultures where fixed stages in the grieving process were laid out. The soul of the dead person only left forty days after the body had breathed its last. Only then was the departed gone for good. With this story and similar ones he'd been able to soothe the mourners time and again. Distract and lead them into a labyrinth of consolation. Even though as a student he'd been too young to be taken on as a funeral orator, he'd soon made a name for himself. Word got around about the quality of his speeches. The work suited him. His manner, at once reserved and empathetic, made him a much sought-after orator, and, to his surprise, he was able to make a decent living of it.

But now that he was on the other end of things, his expert knowledge wasn't any help. Does the soul leave the body forty days after death? There was no way he could struggle with that for so long. Driving himself crazy here wasn't helping anyone. Nor would it bring the electrician back to life. Although still worried that being quick to pay would suggest a bad conscience, buried guilt, he went to the bank the next morning. He was only going to drop off his donation at Elektro Janko. They could pass the money on to the widow later, at a time of their choosing.

By the entrance he withdrew five hundred euros. When the ATM asked what denominations he wanted, Escher was stumped. Personally, he preferred smaller denominations, as more and more shops were put out when they saw a large note. But there was something ostentatious about a thick envelope full of small notes. Then again, smaller denominations would surely be handier for the widow. He must not, just because of some idea of envelope etiquette or excessive discretion, expose her to those shameless shopkeepers who glared at you when you paid with a hundred-euro note. On the other hand, his notes would be lumped together with all the donations from the firm. Might the boss perhaps exchange the notes before handing them to the widow because she shared Escher's concerns?

The ATM spat out five one-hundred euro notes. Even though he was on top of his finances, he was surprised each time the machine actually gave him money. He'd never needed a loan, had never borrowed from a friend or even overdrawn. Funeral orators earned more than you'd expect. Mourners were often so loose with their money that you almost had to protect them from their own generosity. At any rate, it was enough for Escher's lifestyle. As he practically spent nothing—the rent was cheap and acquiring puzzles his only luxury—he was easily able to make ends meet.

He'd even invested in a pension plan. He didn't tell anyone this last fact because he found it embarrassing that he'd already started thinking about this as a student. And in truth it hadn't really been his intention. But who would have believed that he'd bought the shares to get rid of the money? The value of his shares had halved in the first week, and as they continued to plunge, he soon stopped bothering with them.

This embarrassing saga dated back to his time as a fledgling funeral orator. To his surprise a publishing house had offered him an advance of ten thousand marks for his thinly veiled diary, which he'd sent out under the title *A Sad Affair*. He hadn't been expecting an offer—after all, he was a nobody. He signed the contract as soon as he received it, sending it back that very same day. If the book sold in quantities that surpassed the ten-thousand-mark advance, he would be entitled to his respective royalties. Theoretically you could earn millions this way, granted, only if your book sold in the millions.

The author received 8 percent. His share of each book pretty much amounted to one mark. If sales were healthy, his share would rise accordingly, first to 1.10, then 1.20 marks. That was the publisher's arrangement. In the process he found out that half of the retail price went to the bookshop. The rest went to the publisher, who used the money to recoup the production and marketing costs. The one mark he got made the calculation simple: The first ten thousand books would earn out his advance of ten thousand marks. Then a real killing could be made.

A Sad Affair turned out to be a flop, however. Only 347 copies made it past the register. For the publisher it was a net loss. The fact that Escher didn't need to pay back the advance was scant consolation. He found it embarrassing and wanted to be free of the ten thousand marks as soon as possible. He hid his hurt that nobody was interested in *A Sad Affair* behind another slight. Very much against type, he burst into a furious tirade, lambasting the fact that the capitalists raked in the lion's share of the book price, while only a measly 8 percent was left for the author. It was just like Big Dairy, where farmers received a mere fraction of the retail price of their milk. What sort of a world was that?

The young Escher freed himself from this emotional turmoil with a grandiose gesture. Taking a popular saying to heart—that the smart criminal founded a bank rather than robbed one—he used the ten thousand marks he'd received for his book to buy shares in a large book retailer. Rather than being so stupid as to write a book, you should get involved in bookselling. With an amateur understanding of the stock market, he bought the shares purely out of spite, because *A Sad Affair* had been such a flop.

In the weeks and months that followed, the shares fell dramatically. In the newspaper it was reported that the company he'd invested in had accrued nothing but debt and would soon be filing for bankruptcy. It was a money drain that incurred only losses. Although the shares, as the finance pages said, had a lot of imagination, the company had no basis in reality. This Potemkin bookseller didn't even have any brick-and-mortar shops; you ordered everything online and then the book came by mail.

Burning through his advance made Escher feel unburdened. Just as in many cultures dead people were given unbelievable treasures to take with them into the afterlife, he sank the ten thousand marks with the book. It was an exculpation, an exorcism through which he put behind him his humiliating attempt to become a writer.

Since then he had been content with his lot. As if the flop had toughened him up, he also stopped writing down his experiences altogether. He liked his job. A meaningful and stable career without major price fluctuations. The only thing that had stayed with him from his student days was the surprise he felt whenever the ATM handed him money without hesitation. Escher put the cash into an envelope, slipped this into his jacket pocket, and made his way to Elektro Janko. It was a pleasant half-hour's walk. Once there, however, he discovered that something so old-fashioned as a lunch break still existed, which is why he strained against the locked door in vain.

It appeared to be Elektro Janko's intention to try his patience. Half of the lunch hour was over, at least, so Escher took a seat on a bench in a nearby park to wait out the rest. Fortunately, he'd remembered to bring his book.

On August 14, 2007, Marko finished the Vespa. He'd have loved to have worked on it for longer, but try as he might, he was unable to find a single piece he hadn't restored or replaced. Now he could take his first ride. His resolve never to be seen with it in public had weakened over time. He even took it for a quick spin around his workshop without a helmet. Then reason triumphed and, for his first proper ride, he donned a helmet, as prescribed by law. It was the first time he'd worn a helmet since his ride on Falcone's Laverda.

The Vespa gripped the road beautifully. It didn't go half as fast as the Laverda and the police didn't stop him.

The empty tank did.

To be so unlucky. To suffer a setback. To run into an obstacle.

When Marko Steiner got angry he didn't count to one hundred, he ran through his studied compendium of vocabulary.

Banger! Rust bucket! Charlatan! Bungler! Botcher! Dilettante! Quack!

Marko Steiner cursed himself for his sloppy assembly of the fuel line, which, as he discovered only now by the side of the road, was leaking fuel.

To have more luck than judgment. The luck of the devil. As luck would have it.

To his relief he realized that he would have to push the Vespa only one hundred yards until the road started sloping downward. And at the end of this freewheeling powered by gravity he could already spy a gas station.

The BP gas station in Neudorf was very well looked after. Even the toilet paper dispenser was full, and Marko could wipe down the greasy bits where the gas had dribbled out. He also managed to push the hose into the clip so that the problem could be solved by borrowing a screwdriver from behind the counter.

The old man at the register beamed at him. "Nobody minds pushing a thoroughbred like that for a bit, do they, eh?"

"My own fault," Marko said. "I botched it."

"You don't often see a Primavera in such good condition these days," the old man said, refusing to allow his good mood to be dampened. "I used to have one myself. In green! But that was a long time ago."

Marko left before the old man launched into another nostalgic aside about old mopeds, which he knew was only too likely. But the first admirers had gathered outside too. Two guys in dark sunglasses were inspecting the Vespa. Although neither said a word, Marko could tell where they came from by how they carried themselves and dressed. Despite the heat they were outfitted in elegant suits as if on their way to a wedding or coming from a funeral. The Vespa suited them as much as the sunglasses and highly polished ankle boots.

To avoid his compatriots Marko took a detour via the gas station bathroom. A thorough wash wouldn't hurt his hands, which he'd given only a cursory rinse after repairing the fuel hose.

When he got back he realized that taking his time hadn't helped. On the contrary, the younger of the two men was now sitting on the Vespa.

Filthy paws. Mitts. Claws. Trotters.

Marko Steiner stopped briefly and watched the two of them from a safe distance. The idiot posing on the Vespa had a pimply baby face and was much younger than the brawny chrome dome beside him. Instead of a shirt and tie like the younger one, the baldie sported a red T-shirt beneath his rather tight jacket. He was twice as broad as the boy, shorter, and his head was decorated with several tattoos.

Marko heard pimply face say in Italian to chrome dome, "Let's take it with us now."

As he approached the two men, Marko put on his helmet.

"Is this yours?" baldie asked in German.

Marko nodded. With the helmet on it felt as if he were launching into a headbutt. He could see himself in the man's sunglasses. He wore wrap-around lenses. Not only did he have the build of a boxer, on his T-shirt was a picture of the legendary champion Primo Carnera.

"How much?" he asked Marko.

"Tell him we'll pay more than the piece of junk is worth," pimply face said to the boxer in Italian. He was wearing rimless shades with gold arms. GUCCI was engraved on the upper edge of the right lens.

"I'll pay him a thousand and *basta*."

"I've got to get going now," Marko said, gesturing to the buffoon in the GUCCI shades that he should get off his Vespa.

"How much?" the boxer asked in German. "I'm buying."

"It's not for sale," Marko said flipping down his visor.

"A grand."

Shaking his head, Marko reached for the handlebars. But the douche made no move to get off.

The boxer flipped up Marko's visor and spoke into the helmet as if through a box-office window. "Eleven hundred!"

As this movement made the tight jacket open even more, Marko was able to read the quotation beneath the portrait of the boxer on the man's muscular chest: *La vita è merda, pugni e sangue. Nessuno ti regala niente.*

He couldn't help laughing.

"What are you laughing at? You're getting eleven hundred euros for an old wreck of a Vespa and a lifetime supply of pizza at Pizzeria da Bruno."

"Where's the pizzeria?"

"Just around the corner from here—46 Mülheimer Strasse— by the station," the boy said.

"That's no good to me. I don't live here," Marko explained, pretending not to understand pimply face, who remarked in Italian, "The idiot doesn't understand what's going on!"

Slaphead reached into his inside jacket pocket and pulled

out a golden clasp holding a wad of banknotes. With that natural deftness of hulks that Marko had been familiar with since childhood, he counted off eleven hundred marks in a flash and held them out. "Final offer. Take it. We need the Vespa. For a birthday present."

Marko nodded and told the boy to fetch a screwdriver from inside the shop to take off the license plate. The moment he got off the moped, Marko leaped on and rode off. Three-Card Monte, he recalled, cursing the fact that the Primavera didn't have a rearview mirror. Dodge. Ruse. Wile. Ploy. Knowhow!

Ten hours later six people were shot dead at Pizzeria da Bruno, 46 Mülheimer Strasse. It was the lead news story across all the channels. A family had gathered at the Italian restaurant for a birthday party. After midnight the guests left the pizzeria in two cars.

"The birthday boy didn't survive his eighteenth. Marko Tomaso was sitting in the blue VW Golf with Pforzheim plates, which was as badly riddled with bullets as the white Opel delivery van with Duisburg plates. This horrific crime totaled six deaths. All of them men from Calabria."

On one image it was possible to make out the T-shirt of one of the dead men, which showed the face of the boxer Primo Carnera. With a doleful expression on her face, the newsreader read out the T-shirt's platitude: "Life consists of shit, blood, and fists. Nobody gives you anything." Then she looked at Marko Steiner again as if he had done something wrong.

The T-shirt gave the police their first lead. A gas station attendant recognized it. He was very eager to give a statement. The

CCTV footage during his shift showed two of the murdered men striking a deal with an unknown Vespa driver. Fortunately, Marko had his helmet on, and because he had put the Primavera to one side to carry out the repair, the license plate wasn't in the frame.

Marko Steiner disassembled the Vespa into more than one hundred pieces and took them to the scrapyard. He hawked his bicycles and spare parts way below market value to his permanently stoned fellow gearheads at Bikin' in the Wind. Five days after the murders he risked the trip to the train station. Finally, he followed Falcone's advice and moved to the biggest city in the country. Although the police regarded the killings as a purely Italian matter on German soil, they were still checking every single passenger five days later. They were utterly fastidious and were making their way to his seat so slowly that Marko almost went mad. To calm himself he fetched his book from the suitcase and started reading.

Escher's plan did not survive the lunch break. Before it was over he'd already changed his mind. Although he would happily be rid of the cash he'd withdrawn, he did not now go to see Frau Janko in the office. As he waited on the park bench, a new plan took shape. Escher wanted to do the oration at the electrician's funeral. That, he felt, was the best way to atone for his misdeed. For a moment or two it had seemed like a ludicrous idea, because he was too bound up with the tragic accident. But now he thought it feasible. Under the right circumstances. He just had to orchestrate it correctly. Preferably through a colleague, without trying too hard to land the job himself.

It was fairly common for funeral orators to swap gigs. If there were scheduling issues, they helped each other out. The only problem was that Escher wasn't especially popular among his colleagues. Although he wasn't in open conflict like the retired teacher Walcher, who undercut everyone else, or the Dutchman Van Heel, who bribed the undertakers beyond the collectively negotiated commission. But ever since the debut of his novel about funeral orators, Escher had found the others treated him warily. Even though the book had been published in the previous century! His older colleagues, those who'd been around at the time, still made it clear that they didn't trust him. The younger ones, too, showed a certain reserve toward Escher. He didn't think these whippersnappers knew anything about his book—the subject wasn't good fodder. It was more that the mistrust had been passed down to the next generation. Possibly it was his own behavior that, anticipating mistrust, gave rise to it. But maybe these negative feelings toward him had long since vanished into thin air and he merely sensed them as a phantom pain.

Right after publication, however, it had been anything but his imagination.

His work almost ground to a halt. Some undertakers openly boycotted him, and had his orations not been superior to the more predictable offerings of his colleagues, thereby securing him sufficient word-of-mouth recommendations from the clientele-in-mourning, he surely would have had to find other means of employment.

These experiences had put Escher on guard, and so he decided not to ask his colleagues but instead phoned the funeral directors, disabling his caller ID and using a false name. He began with Blunt, who, as the other funeral orators liked to joke, wasn't the sharpest tool in the shed.

"Hello, Elektro Janko here," Escher introduced himself. "I've got a question. It's about our colleague who died in an accident. I believe you're looking after the funeral arrangements?"

"Name?"

The undertaker got in a tizzy when Escher confessed he didn't know the dead man's name. He was only ringing on behalf of the firm, he stammered. But when the undertaker couldn't find anything under the company's name, he became nervous and called out something impatiently to a colleague. Escher hung up. Blunt had always been an odd bundle of nerves. Why opt for a career like that if it didn't lead to a certain serenity? He tried two other funeral directors with his half-baked strategy. But the name Electro Janko didn't ring a bell with them either.

It dawned on Escher that he needed to come up with a better idea. Maybe it was more sensible to arrange it directly via his colleagues after all. The one he knew best, of course, was Nellie Wieselburger, MA. But he was not keen on asking her for a favor. Things were a bit tricky with her. At the time his book was published she'd been the only person who actually had good reason to be insulted. And yet, of all of them, she'd been very relaxed about the book and hadn't made him feel he'd done anything wrong. Through this, a sort of debt of obligation had developed between the two of them.

Although she'd complained vociferously that she was called Mitzi Stiegl, MA, in Escher's novel, she'd brushed all other qualms aside.

"Mitzi for Nellie," she'd confronted him angrily. "That's just pure spite! I'll never forgive you that, Escher."

Behind this manufactured outrage, he could already sense a willingness to reconcile. At any rate it was far more innocuous than the whisperings of his colleagues who'd let him know that the name Mitzi was not the real reason for Nellie Wieselburger's indignation. She wouldn't admit it, they claimed, but what she felt most insulted by was the surname Stiegl. Surely everybody understood that the character in the novel was named after Stiegl beer, an allusion to Wieselburger beer. It was obvious that an art historian with her family pedigree would rather be associated with the aristocratic distinction of "Burg" and "Wiesel" and coats of arms, rather than with the insipid taste of lager. "Mitzi" wasn't the problem, it was "Stiegl."

As far as Escher was concerned, either grievance was equally senseless. The truth was simpler, as it was in every argument. You talk about everything apart from the real issue. Nellie never complained that Escher's novel had made her funeral orations out to be insubstantial and gimmicky, something she justifiably could have felt insulted by. His phrase "always cobbled together from the same building blocks of condolence" seemed to bounce right off her. Nor had he been able to refrain from putting Nellie's favorite word into Mitzi's mouth every couple of lines. *Empathy*! The first time Escher had ever encountered the term *empathy* it was from Nellie Wieselburger. Soon he was hearing it all the time. *Empathy* was rampant. In all likelihood there was a direct correlation to the widespread devaluing of the word's meaning. This would explain why "empathy" clung permanently to the lips of those who didn't possess normal human compassion in the slightest. Emotional cripples would brandish their "empathy" crutches above their heads at every possible opportunity, and Nellie's funeral orations were never without the word. That's how it was and that's what it said in his book, too. One critic even remarked positively that this was a rare instance where the author's polemic worked. But it wasn't a polemic, it was plain fact.

Nellie had never reproached him for any of this. She didn't once bring up the way he'd described her funeral orations or portrayed her as a heartless automaton. She'd gotten worked up only about the name Mitzi. Escher was sorry that the nickname Mitzi then stuck for good among their colleagues. An astonishing impact, when you think that only 347 copies were sold.

Fortunately, all that was long in the past and much grass had grown over it since. Glaciers had flowed down the Danube; graves had been dug and later abandoned; and now, Escher decided to risk it all. Perhaps Nellie Wieselburger, carried away by empathy, would help him out. To his astonishment he no longer had her number in his contacts. But there it was, staring him in the face, on her website. Escher was distracted, though, by the graphics. Before he could type in her number, he first had to get over the fact that her home page displayed *Madonna with the Long Neck*. Nothing was too stupid for her. He wondered whether this really was a good idea, but then he got his act together and gave her a call.

"You've reached Nellie Wieselburger, MA, bereavement counselor," her voice plaintively announced. "I'm sorry I can't take your call at the moment, but I'll get back to you promptly. Please leave a message aft—"

Escher hung up without leaving a message. The term *bereavement counselor* made him go limp. And what was "promptly" supposed to mean? Gazing at *Madonna with the Long Neck*, which he'd assembled so often, he pondered whether to ring the number again. But he was pretty sure she'd return his call soon anyway. And while he waited for her to phone, he could read another few pages.

The shed where Marko opened his new bicycle workshop was so far from the center of this vast capital city that he felt as if he'd moved to the backwaters. The hut transformed almost overnight into a workshop. It took a while for the shop to get going, which suited him fine, but customers eventually started trickling in. The newest trend on the bicycle market very much suited Marko's talents. He no longer restored old racers but now specialized in e-bikes. Marko Steiner loved electric motors. In his former life he had dismantled, converted and rebuilt hundreds of them. For the boss of bosses, not only had he manned the drones that facilitated his escape, but his surveillance system had made the hideaway where the boss now lived more secure than a high-security prison.

Word of an e-bike wiz soon got around. Among e-bike freaks

the Steiner tuning rapidly acquired a mythical status comparable to that enjoyed by Schnitzer, Abarth, or AMG among couch potatoes in their four-wheeled lounges. Marko Steiner had always scorned anything on four wheels. When one day a woman turned up with a problem with her ten-year-old Golf, he immediately dismissed her: "I'm afraid I don't do cars."

First, it was already evening; second, Marko didn't touch cars on principle; and third, the fact that the woman bore some resemblance to Isa Neri, Falcone's assistant, who to Marko's chagrin had one day moved to Rome, disappearing out of his sight forever, didn't change anything.

"It's just a problem with the alarm."

Fourth, he didn't like her supercilious tone. Self-assured. Certain of victory. Brash, brasher, brashest. Bold, bolder, boldest. Sassy, sassier, sassiest. Or was it sassyer/sassyest?

Fifth, he'd never liked it when someone stood there as if they were Isa Neri in the flesh.

"I'm afraid I don't do cars," he reiterated calmly.

"Strictly speaking the alarm isn't the car," she negotiated. "It's an electrical system."

Sixth, if someone thought they had to explain to him what electrical systems were, that was the end of the line.

Trying his best to avoid making eye contact, he stared disapprovingly at her Golf. He had to tread lightly. Although she was younger than Isa Neri, she radiated a classical beauty. She looked how women used to look. Back home. And she wasn't actually brash. She just had that way about her. Seventh, he certainly wasn't going to touch a car just because a woman had that way about her.

"Nah," he said, turning back to the e-bike he wanted to have finished by the following morning.

"No?"

He shook his head.

She laughed.

Eighth, not even if she laughed like that.

Without looking up from the bike, he said, "Working on alarm systems will drive you to drink. Besides, I can't get under the vehicle, I don't have a grease pit."

"Georgi says you can do anything."

Ninth, he'd never been susceptible to flattery. He hadn't even believed the boss when he declared he'd never seen such a work of art as the camera in the eye of the stone Madonna.

"Georgi?"

"Georgi says you're a miracle worker."

"I don't know any Georgi."

"I bet he'll be pleased when he hears that. Georgi from Men of Many Parts!"

As it turned out, his contact at the spare-part supplier Men of Many Parts had a name. He was called Georgi. For Marko he was just "office" at Men of Many Parts, but for her he was Georgi, her friend's brother.

"My friend says, why don't you talk to Georgi? And Georgi says, why don't you talk to Marko Steiner?"

"The guy's name is Georgi?"

"That damn alarm is driving me up the wall!"

"Whenever I call the office he always answers with Hans-Georg."

"Of course. Georgi and Hans-Georg are one and the same. Only Georgi doesn't sound as silly as Hans-Georg."

"What's your name?"

"I already told you. Gabriele."

Marko Steiner laughed.

"What's so funny?"

"That sounds silly too."

He was satisfied with this response. Marko knew he mustn't repeat her name. Words shared in common with his old language were always a problem. Although he'd finally accepted that there were women here with the man's name Gabriele, for the life of him he couldn't retch a German "Gabriele" from his throat, like a bird regurgitating worms for her young. Retrofitting an old bicycle into an e-bike was child's play, but it was impossible to make the jump from his cousin Annunziata-Gabriela, whose father was buried in the underground garage of the school, to a strangled pharyngeal Gabriele.

"You can call me Gabi."

He didn't call her anything. Gabi didn't suit her. Annunziata would have been right.

"I do e-bikes. I don't remove alarm systems," he said. "You need to find an auto electrician."

"I've already been to three!" she snapped. "None of them want to take out the alarm. Too much work! They say it's more work than the old clunker's worth."

"Yes," Marko said. "I'm afraid they're right."

"So what am I to do now?"

Marko ruminated. The alarm system was her problem. Gabi was his problem.

"Even the slightest gust of wind sets it off!"

Because Marko merely nodded silently, she sang him the entire lament. Twice last week the police had gotten her out of bed because her Golf had woken the entire street, once at two in the morning and once at four. And nobody wanted to take out the alarm system. Every auto electrician repeated the same line: The whole point of an alarm system was that you couldn't dismantle it. At least not without great effort. It would take many hours. The alarm system was integrated into all possible and impossible parts of the car via a network of cables like a spider's web. A mind-numbing job, hours of having your ears battered by the relentless wail of the alarm. There was nothing you could do.

"Jens also said that if there's anyone who can do it, it's Marko."

"Who's Jens?"

"You know, Sparepartner Jens."

"I only know him as Worldwide Sparepartner J."

"Yes, *J* stands for Jens. My ex-boyfriend. He and Georgi used to run Men of Many Parts. But they had a falling-out, so now he runs Sparepartner Jens and Georgi's Man of Many Parts."

"Sparepartner J," Marko corrected her. "Not Jens. Worldwide Sparepartner J."

"Yeah, yeah, he's such a show-off. The 'Worldwide' bit is just to piss Georgi off. But I get on well with both of them. They're two different types. Or too similar, depending on how you look at it. But both told me I should forget auto electricians. Both said you could do it."

Marko Steiner set his tool on the ground, crossed his arms, and gave a speech: "Your best bet would be to rent a garage. That way your car would be protected from the wind. And at night you wouldn't have any drunks leaning against it. And if the alarm did go off, no one would be there to complain."

He watched her process this interesting suggestion. Rent a garage. Gabs. He could say Gabi. But he'd rather call her something else. Sadly, all the pet names that suited her came from his old life. Insults and pet names. They didn't exist in his new language.

"What are you thinking about?" she asked.

Tenth, Marko thought. Tenth. He looked away from her and gaped at her car as if he were vetting it. Tenth.

"Do you want to wait or come back later?"

"What are you saying?"

He didn't say anything.

"Does that mean you'll do it?"

At that moment Gabriele couldn't have known that she would repeat some variation of these two formulations—"what are you saying" and "does that mean"—many more times over the coming years.

Marko responded to this first "does that mean" inquiry with a faint shrug while imperceptibly cocking his head on a scale of millimeters, as if registering doubts about his own decision as well as the feasibility of the task. But this didn't alter the fact that he'd actually and foolishly said, "Yes."

"Does that mean you can do it right now?" Gabi asked.

"Right now?"

"I *like* your can-do attitude!"

Marko appeared to be deep in thought, as if working out how the same word, *like*, could mean that someone both looked similar to Falcone's assistant, Isa Neri, and was partial to something.

"How long will I have to wait, roughly?"

"That depends," Marko said.

She realized she shouldn't disturb him anymore; he was already at work. Marko pressed his right foot sideways against the right mudguard. The horrific alarm was set off by the first, gentlest touch.

"God! I really hate that alarm!" Gabi cursed, silencing it with her key.

At that moment Marko rammed the patient with a coordinated shove of the hip and elbow, and once more the alarm sounded. No sooner had Gabi turned it off than it wailed again because Marko was yanking the roof rail.

"Should I keep silencing it or let it keep going?"

It was so loud that he couldn't understand her. This time, she chose to let it blare and moved back a few yards, but because the distance and the tree behind which she'd taken cover didn't make the alarm any more bearable, she silenced it yet again.

"Should I be letting it blare or turning it off?"

"Turning it off. I just need to see."

Grabbing the car by the edge of the roof, he used all his strength to pull it toward him, then sent it back into the arms of gravity, which returned it with so much momentum that he was able to pull it even farther toward him and push it away again. Gabi was amazed that this man had the strength to make her car rock. The heavy vehicle pitched and tossed in his hands like a ship in a storm. It reminded her of that heady feeling on a children's swing, of increasing the momentum at exactly the right time to get ever higher.

While this memory washed over Gabi, sending her back in time, Marko Steiner momentarily forgot himself too.

"*Mia cara*," he whispered tenderly to the box of metal he was rocking, inaudible to his client. As he gradually increased the momentum, he whispered even more softly, "*Tesoruccio*," and then pushed even harder and was just forming his lips into a mischievous "*Passerotto*," when he was interrupted by the alarm.

As soon as Gabi, whose name was Gabriele, but who really was more an Isa or Annunziata, had silenced the noise, he set about the vehicle again. Once it was in motion he didn't need to use much force. It was almost as if the Golf, like the sea, had its own waves to rock it.

"*Amoruccio!*"

"*Principessa!*"

The rocking became more and more intense by itself.

"*Dolcissima!*"

You just had to give yourself over to the swelling rhythm.

"*Pupa mia!*"

"Piccola mia!"

"Angioletto!"

"Sciatu meu!"

"Sangu miu!"

Until the one-and-a-half-ton chassis had rocked itself into such lightness that the alarm began to sing.

"It depends on whether you'd like me to preserve the alarm system when I take it out, or break it," he said, finally answering her question. "If you want to sell it, maybe on eBay you can—"

"Destroy that wicked thing," she said, sounding deathly serious.

Marko couldn't help but laugh.

Years later he claimed, "That was the moment I fell in love with you. When you got all worked up and said, 'wicked thing.'"

His claim was a lie, however. It sounded good, but he'd made it up. Maybe it was just wishful thinking. To appear less vulnerable to himself. He knew full well that he'd fallen in love the moment she stepped out of the car and said "Hello." For Gabi there was no doubt when she'd fallen in love. Not the moment he said "Hello." She hadn't fallen in love with him until an hour and a half later when both of them made sure that the alarm wouldn't go off even if the car was given the most powerful thrashing imaginable. Not even during a strain test exceeding every EU norm, undertaken by two bodies that were in perfect sync inside the cramped space of a VW Golf.

After the shaking test (for a moment the two of them thought the alarm had gone off again but it was just an auditory illusion) they came to the sober realization that one ought to talk a bit afterward.

"You're never to ask me any questions," Gabi said.

"Nor you me."

"Let's grab a bite to eat. I'm starving."

"Ravenous," Marko said. "Could eat a horse. Fill the belly."

"Exactly."

"I just need to clear up here first."

The thousand bits of cable from the alarm system were still scattered across the floor, and it bothered Marko when things were untidy.

"I could help."

"No!"

She couldn't know that to Marko, help and being disturbed while working were one and the same.

"It won't take me long. In the meantime make yourself comfortable."

"You've got your T-shirt on the wrong way. Doubly wrong, in fact. It's inside out and back to front!"

She was relieved to see that this man could laugh at himself too.

He invited her to take his tiny seat in the workshop, and because the tidying up took a bit longer than expected, she looked around his strange combination of workshop, camp, and shed. This orderly man appeared to have few secrets. Besides the tools and a drawer full of pens, insulating tape, rubber bands, pencils, and paper clips, there were just a couple of bills and a Man of

Many Parts price list. A book was festering on a windowsill. As he cleared up outside she leafed through it. Where her savior had dog-eared a page she began to read.

The funeral orator Escher was sitting on a park bench when his colleague returned his call.

"So?" the caller greeted him.

Escher hated this "So?" She didn't necessarily have to say her name as he had done. That might be considered a bit old-fashioned. But "So?" was the most idiotic of all possibilities.

"Nice website you've got," he said.

Of course, he could pretend he knew nothing about the picture on her site. This would have been better, in any case. But he had to counter the stupid "So?" with something.

"I know," she said neutrally, as if *Madonna with the Long Neck* had nothing whatsoever to do with them.

"Actually you haven't got a long neck at all," Escher said. "You've got a beautiful nape. That sums it up better."

"I know," she said. "What can I do for you?"

"I wanted to ask you something," Escher said.

She gave a sarcastic laugh.

"But now you don't want to anymore?"

How this manner of hers got on his nerves! This flippant, brattish humor! But he managed to swallow his anger. "Yes, I do. But it's a bit . . . Actually it's totally harmless, but it's a bit complicated. Okay, it's not harmless, but—"

"Is it complex or complicated?"

"Actually, it's not complicated."

"Try me. I'm quick on the uptake."

"Yes," Escher said, refraining from telling her that people who were quick on the uptake often ended up paying a high price for this, because although they always grasped things quickly, they never properly checked them. But they could have argued half the night about that. So why bother bringing that up? She wouldn't check it.

Instead, he told her straight out about the death in his apartment.

"*O mein Gott!*" Nellie exclaimed.

"Have you been watching a lot of American television series recently?"

"Why?"

"Well, the phrase '*O mein Gott*' doesn't actually exist in German. It's just a mistranslation of 'Oh my God' from a Netflix series."

He tried to make "Oh my Gaaaad!" sound as stupid as possible.

"That's not true!" Nellie Wieselburger insisted. "I've always said '*O mein Gott.*' Long before Netflix. I don't watch Netflix anyway. And even if I did, I watch shows in their original language."

"Then you must have picked it up indirectly."

He was shocked by the unrestrained relish with which he stupidly accused her. After all, he wanted something from Nellie. In his attempt to make up for it, he immediately fell into the next trap: pontificating like a know-it-all.

"It's understandable they'd mistranslate it to lip sync the dub. But in reality '*O mein Gott!*' doesn't exist in German. Nobody ever used to say '*O mein Gott!*' Not a single person. If, in the past, someone was frightened, they'd likely cry, '*O Gott!*' And if they were irritated or annoyed, which is a completely different situation, they'd say '*Mein Gott!*' But nobody ever said '*O mein Gott!*' Nobody!"

"*Mein Gott!*" Nellie Wieselburger gasped into the phone.

"It's a mash-up of two completely different expressions. Recently I heard a sports commentator say, 'At the end of the day, it's the early bird that catches the worm.'"

"Well, that's obviously wrong," the magnanimous Nellie agreed. "I mean, the bird can't be early if it's the end of the day."

"Precisely. And in German 'Oh my God' is similar."

"How about 'Oh my God, forgive us our sins, protect us from hell's fire, lead all souls to heaven, especially those most in need of Your mercy'?"

As funeral orators, both were well-acquainted with prayers. Only Nellie had made a little mistake here. Escher was pleased at the opportunity to bring his dogmatism to an end. He just needed to allow himself this minor victory to establish a good starting point to discuss the matter in hand.

"It goes 'Oh my Jesus, forgive us our sins.' Not 'Oh my God,'" he heard himself say. He couldn't believe how pedantic he always felt when he talked to Nellie Wieselburger. For some reason no conversation with Nellie ever went normally.

She laughed as if she knew that he hadn't actually wanted to say that but was unable keep his trap shut. It was a number of years ago now that she'd hurled a few things at him—views, opinions, psychobabble. Ever since then he'd known perfectly well that he had to be on his guard with her, and that's precisely why he kept providing her with confirmation of her prejudices. Because he found even her manner provocative.

"Is that why you rang?" she asked cheerfully. "To tell me that?"

"Look, the thing is, I'd like to give the oration at his funeral."

"The electrician's?"

"Yes, of course. But I'm worried that's not what the widow wants."

"Why not?"

"Well, to begin with she might not ask for an orator at all. And if she does, then not the guy who reminds her of the tragic accident."

"So you're asking me to get the job and then pass it on to you because I can't make it in person?"

Escher had to admit that Nellie's quickness on the uptake had certainly saved him a lot of explaining.

"Yes, if you can bear it."

"Sure, why not. I mean, I'd do the same if I were to blame for the death of a tradesman."

"I'm not to blame! He didn't switch—"

Nellie laughed. "Little joke, Eschi. So, who should I call?"

He explained that it would be best to go through the firm. Elektro Janko. The boss was supporting the widow and would likely be prepared to cover the fee for a funeral orator too.

"But the fee's coming to me," Nellie said.

"If you like."

"You're giving the speech out of guilt. You can't accept a fee for that."

"I don't have anything to feel guilty about."

"Even if you're not directly to blame, you've definitely got feelings of guilt. I would too if I were in your shoes. If you hadn't called for an electrician, he would still be alive. It's natural to feel guilty."

"I'm not going to talk myself into believing that. But I'm happy for you to have the money."

"I'll just do it through my company."

"Company," Escher said neutrally, although he thought it ridiculous to describe a single-person household as a "company."

"What?"

"Yes, through the company. That's fine. Now you've got your first colleague."

"We don't say 'colleague' these days," Nellie said.

"What, then?"

"Underling. Or slave."

"Ha, ha," Escher said, drawing it out slightly to allow her the little joke, but also so he could throw it back at her. "Call her now. She's in the office. The lunch break has just finished."

"Will do."

Before he could ask her to ring him back afterward, she'd already hung up. This probably meant she was already phoning Elektro Janko. Not only was she quick on the uptake, she was also decisive and did things in a jiffy.

Escher, on the other hand, was completely exhausted by their conversation. It was the exhaustion of someone returning home from a journey through time to an antiquated form of existence where one still wasted the sort of energy that could destroy a planet to maintain human contact with people like Nellie Wieselburger.

Five minutes later Nellie still hadn't called back. Not even after ten. He wondered whether he ought to phone and press her. Whether to shoot a "What's going on?" over the phone. It would probably be better to wait a while longer. In truth, he was someone who was good at waiting. Maybe she hadn't been able to get through to the boss straightaway. Maybe the phone was always engaged at Elektro Janko. Perhaps Nellie Wieselburger was stuck on hold and would never get out.

He reached again for the book that lay open beside him on the park bench. Marko never revealed his true identity to Gabi, never told her the words he'd whispered to her car, and, most important, never let show the pain it caused him every time she said her name, "Gabriele." In the same fashion, she never let on that her name wasn't actually Gabriele. Having, in this way, safely guarded their secrets, and because they got on so well, they were soon married after only six months. During this six-month lead-up Gabi never once asked after his family or about his childhood. Not even his favorite dish. Marko Steiner had quickly realized that he had found the One. His desire to marry her grew with every passing day that she asked him nothing. Out of respect, he didn't ask her anything either, apart from whether she would marry him.

"Of course. But who will we have as witnesses?'"

"Georgi from Man of Many Parts?" Marko suggested.

"He can be mine," Gabi said. "And you can take Sparepartner Jens. That way the two of them will be forced to make up."

The wedding was carefree and jolly. The only casualty was Sparepartner Jens, who, in discovering that he was allergic to wine and beer, so overdid his "gin-only" diet that for the next three days he was unable to take orders or send packages. They hadn't noticed much during the wedding celebration besides a slight slur when Jens was toasting his old friend, whose name was reinterpreted by the gin into something that slid off the tongue more easily: Shorshie. One might have gotten the impression that Marko and Gabriele had been invited as witnesses to the two men's great reconciliation. The next day, however, Jens couldn't remember that he'd made up with Georgi, but when he saw the drunken pictures from the wedding there was no going back.

Gabi and Marko had a wild time too, without having to struggle with any memory lapses. And certainly no lapses when it came to their secrets. Neither before, during, nor after the ceremony did either party let anything slip. Marko was just surprised that Gabriele was taking his name. "You don't have to do it for my sake," he'd protested on the morning of the wedding. "I'm not that old-fashioned."

"There's nothing nicer than shedding your name," Gabi had said. And in some way, he was pleased that the name she was taking wasn't his real one.

It goes without saying that Gabi and Marko's union was

harmonious. She never asked, What are you thinking?, nor
did he ever ask, What are you thinking? She never said, Why
are you looking like that?, nor did he ever say, Why are you
looking like that? In the best way possible it could be said of
this married couple that they weren't interested in each other.
Marko was fascinated by the fact that Gabi intuitively knew
how dangerous it would be to poke around in his past. In this
regard, it was a pure love, unencumbered by a pointless interest in each other.

Gabi had a job with one of the largest industrial firms in
the world. But she'd never seen any machinery or factories full
of robots because she worked in the complaints department.
Marko loved the stories she brought home from work. Gabi
could talk for hours on end, listing off the curious things she
heard over the course of a day. Once, she rather unexpectedly
found herself needing to report a problem she had with one of
the company's products. Unable to file it internally, she ended
up calling the line herself and submitting the complaint to her
colleague at the next desk over. On the off chance she no longer wanted to talk shop, she passed the baton to Marko. His
favorite topic was the various groceries and markets where he'd
shopped for dinner. Like his grandmother, who marked the
days her sons had died by preparing large feasts and serving
their favorite dishes, he never spoke of the actual cooking, only
the ingredients he'd purchased.

As all his dishes supposedly came from Switzerland, he
had to invent new names for them. "Cannelloni Bellinzoni"

was Gabi's favorite, just edging out "Locarno con Carne" and "Sprüngli in Boca" with a sage leaf.

Every night they shared a bottle of Austrian white wine called Field Blend. Marko claimed that Italian wine gave him a headache. Gabi never questioned this. Swiss wine, meanwhile, in Marko's estimation, without ever having tried a sip of it, made people belligerent. On the other hand, Field Blend made people talkative. Quiet by nature, he saw Field Blend as a necessary tool for his survival. For he knew that the more someone had to hide, the more they had to talk. With the help of Field Blend they never tired of each other. And if it ever came to it, Marko could always invent new recipes and Gabi new complaints.

Being quiet, then, was left to their daughter, Ala, born a year into their marriage. She was content with being an observer. If her childish nature drove her to ask a question, she was soon satisfied with an answer. If she asked her father how he'd managed to do something, she did so with the understanding that he'd always answer the same: "Three-Card Monte."

One day, after her mother spotted a man on the other side of the street and hid in panic, Ala thought to wonder why but settled for the first answer she got. Ala was four and she had no reason to doubt her mother's explanation that it was a man who kept coming into the complaints department and getting on everyone's nerves.

"We have to move," Gabi told her husband that evening.

Marko didn't ask why. Ala didn't say anything about the man that afternoon.

"Where to?" Marko asked.

"It doesn't matter, we just need to leave this city. The country, preferably. I can't take it here anymore."

"If you want to move to another country, now's as good a time as ever," Marko reasoned. "Ala will easily pick up a new language by the time she starts school."

"It doesn't have to be a country where they speak a different language," Gabi replied. "What about where you grew up?"

"What?"

"We could move to Switzerland."

"No," Marko said, and he was happy to have a wife who didn't ask why.

Seeing that the food was ready, it occurred to Marko that he had to make a snap judgment. He wanted this matter settled before they sat down to eat. In the second it took him to grab the bottle of wine from the fridge he reached a decision. "How about the birthplace of Field Blend?"

"Done!" Gabi said.

Three days later they were heading south to the country of field blends. They took no more than what could fit into Gabi's old Golf. Not only had she been pleased to shed her name, leaving things behind was a blessing too. Only the essentials came along.

After Marko stomped the last few boxes and stuffed them into the recycling bin, he chucked in the book that the junkie Sven had given him.

"But I haven't finished reading that," his wife protested.

"Nor have I."

Impulsively, she took it out of the bin and stashed it in her handbag.

"If I put it in my bag it won't take up any space in the car," she informed her husband.

"Your mother can work magic," Marko told Ala.

"Three-Card Monte," his wife said.

Gabi was grateful to have a book. It was so hot in this foreign city that there was no way she'd be able to sleep. At midnight it was still seventy-nine degrees. The bed was unfamiliar, the heat was unfamiliar, and the noises were unfamiliar. While Marko and Ala slept deeply, Gabi tossed and turned. Finally, she moved to the sofa in the other room and began to read.

Escher realized that in all the commotion he'd committed a cardinal sin. He'd made himself dependent on Nellie Wieselburger, MA. He could no longer ignore her calls. He had to answer each time she rang. And of course, it was never about the Elektro Janko matter but whatever was on her mind at the moment. Escher didn't understand how someone like Nellie existed. His request for a minor favor wasn't a bid for serfdom.

But on Sunday, May 3, at precisely 2:35 p.m., she finally overplayed her hand. She called and, without further ado, said, "Hey, fancy going for a coffee?"

"Why?" Escher said.

"Why?" Nellie repeated as if he were the most unalluring oaf on God's sweet earth. "Just because!"

"Have you heard anything from Frau Janko?"

"She said she'll call me back next week. It's only Sunday."

"What is it, then?"

"What do you mean, what is it?"

"Well, why are you calling me?"

"Does there have to be a reason to go for a coffee? Look, forget it."

Not wanting to offend her, he resorted to a white lie.

"I can't right now. I'm in the middle of a puzzle."

Nellie Wieselburger laughed out loud. "Do you still play with puzzles?"

"What of it?"

"Don't get your panties in a twist. Actually, I'm laughing for a different reason. Don't you remember?"

"Of course I do," Escher said.

"Extraordinary, how long has it been?"

"A long time."

"Look, don't take this the wrong way," she began.

Escher despised sentences that began with these words. Their meaning completely rested on your taking them the wrong way.

"But I'd really like to," Nellie blurted out. "There's no harm in us playing with a puzzle again together."

He especially didn't like when people said "playing with puzzles." You didn't play with puzzles. You assembled them, put them together, even simply *did* them, but never played.

"I don't know," he said. "You raked me over the coals last time."

Nellie laughed. "Do you know the line, 'You bear grudges and I'm never going to forget that'?"

"It's an old one."

Half an hour later Nellie Wieselburger stood at his door. Her lipstick nearly matched the color of the pastry box she handed him with the words, "I brought us something sweet."

"Cake?" Escher said. "We should eat it afterward. Otherwise, we'll get the puzzle sticky."

"I won't touch anything with my sticky hands."

Escher lamented that he didn't own any one-hundred-piece puzzles. Once, he'd even considered culling all his five-hundred-piece ones but found he didn't have the heart to go through with it. But now his weakness had paid off. Five-hundred-piece puzzles had the advantage that you could spread them out on the table. He didn't particularly fancy crawling around on the floor with Nellie Wieselburger.

She stood by his huge shelves and gasped. "You haven't got any books left! Don't you read anymore?"

"I do, but I give away the books I've read. I need all the space here."

"It's extraordinary how many puzzles you have. How do you find your way around them?"

"Well, I've got a system," he muttered without going into it.

Escher noticed that he had mixed feelings, a situation he found thoroughly disagreeable. Although he was pleased to see her admiring his collection, he also found it a shameless invasion of his privacy.

"Over there you've got all the natural wonders," Nellie deduced. "Marine life, space and that."

"Natural wonders," Escher repeated, but refrained to say why he didn't find the term appropriate.

"And there you've got labyrinths. So many labyrinths, it's depraved. And there's the art."

She turned to the three-yard-long shelves with artworks and shook her head. "It's mad—half of art history as puzzles. Who produces all this? It's really a bit . . . I just can't believe it."

"Pick one," Escher said nobly, absentmindedly opening the cake box, even though he wanted to leave it till later. "But pick one from down there. They're only five hundred pieces. That way we can do it on the table, rather than having to go crawling around on the floor."

"It's got a ring to it, hasn't it?" Nellie laughed childishly. "Would you like to see my puzzle collection? It's a bit like with a stamp collection, isn't it?"

"I'm beyond that age."

"Really? How old are you, in fact?" Escher didn't get to answer because in true Nellie Wieselburger fashion she immediately launched into another question. "But why five hundred pieces? How many have the others got?"

"A thousand."

"Well, I want to do a proper one. I don't mind being on the floor. I often sit on the floor at home."

"Sure, but not in your pencil skirt."

"Pencil skirt!" She laughed again. "Your vocabulary! This isn't a pencil skirt."

As she scanned the shelf with her head cocked, Escher noticed again her exceptionally beautiful neck. If he were being honest, she had the most beautiful neck he'd ever seen. In truth it wasn't just the neck. It began with the shoulders and had a lot to do with the back of her head. Perhaps it was the entire architectural ensemble. It was something abstract, something absent, the curve, detached from the parts that formed it. Escher just hoped she wasn't going to pull out the *Madonna with the Long Neck* puzzle and dredge up the past. In the now-remaindered novel *A Sad Affair*, his alter ego had put together that puzzle with Mitzi Stiegl. Wrongly (he was free to take some creative liberties, after all) he'd claimed that the art historian was writing her dissertation on *Madonna with the Long Neck*. This—besides the name Mitzi—is what had gotten Nellie most worked up, while she conveniently ignored other things. She didn't care that the character Mitzi Stiegl was described as an insanely coquettish woman, who without fail, as she kneeled on the floor, reached for the puzzle pieces in as provocative a manner as possible. Perhaps Nellie sensed that Escher wasn't referring to her with that description, but channeling his old memory of Martine. But she couldn't forgive him the wrong painting. In truth, they'd assembled a completely different picture.

"Here it is," Nellie said, chuckling, as she unerringly pulled *The Beheading of Saint John the Baptist* from the shelf. "Did you buy it again, then?"

So she remembered that she'd borrowed his puzzle and never returned it. Not a word of apology came from her lips, only pity for the man who'd lost his head. "Poor John! That we had such a fight because of him."

"That's water under the bridge," Escher said.

"In the beginning I thought you were joking," Nellie said, embarking—obviously—on the old story again. "You pretended for so long that you hadn't noticed!"

"Why don't we just leave it," Escher suggested. "I mean, we've been over this thousands of times."

"You simply replace *The Beheading of Saint John the Baptist* with *Madonna with the Long Neck*. And then you claim that I'm writing my dissertation on *Madonna with the Long Neck* rather than beheadings!"

"That was just the camouflage. I was doing you a favor! Otherwise, everyone would have recognized it was you because of the dissertation topic. If I'd written . . . What was the exact title again?"

"'Declarations and Decapitations in Painting from 1520 to 1620.' Don't act like you don't remember!"

"Declarations and decapitations. Exactly."

"You told me often enough what a stupid title it was."

Now he recalled the entire disaster in full Technicolor. The Mitzi name hadn't been the only objection on her part. She'd also gotten worked up about this. Swapping *The Beheading of Saint John the Baptist* with *Madonna with the Long Neck* was, as far as Nellie was concerned, a clear case of turning the violence of the decapitation back on her personally. Somebody with a long neck could easily be beheaded; indeed, she posited that Escher's substitution implied that the long neck was crying out to be severed. It was a crystal-clear threat against her person.

At this time, Escher thought, *She's got a screw loose.* But the way he spoke to her was conciliatory. It was only meant as a compliment, he insisted. Surely, she must realize that she didn't have a long neck, just an exceptionally lovely one. At the climax of their argument he snapped, "Give me a break, don't pretend you've no idea that every man stares at your slender neck!"

"How can you say 'break' and 'neck' in the same sentence and not think anything of it?" she exclaimed as quick as a shot. "In a way I think it's a good thing that you're so unaware."

With this final judgment she'd ended the argument, never to return to it.

"I stopped being cross with you ages ago," Nellie now said.

Escher shook his head.

"Anyway, I've changed the topic."

"Are you still writing your dissertation?"

"Absolutely. I'm writing it for myself, so I don't have any time pressure. But I've got another focus now. Beheadings are only the starting point."

"That reassures me," Escher said, but deliberately didn't probe. Maybe he would be spared after all.

"My topic is now generally 'Cutting in Painting.' I'm focusing more on the form now rather than just the content, do you get me?"

"Anything's better than decapitation. That gives me the willies."

"I wouldn't have pegged you for such a wimp," Nellie said. Then, to his relief, she returned the *Beheading* to the shelf and took out *Nativity with Saint Francis and Saint Lawrence*.

"We could do this one," she said.

"If you like."

"It's quite fitting, isn't it? Us putting the picture together. After it was cut up by your Mafia."

"What do you mean 'my Mafia'?"

"You read all that Mafia crap, don't you?" she said, handing him the box.

"That doesn't mean it's *my* Mafia."

"They brutally cut the canvas out of the frame and then into four parts. Imagine! Such vandals!"

"That's just a rumor about the four parts," Escher said, feeling the need to prove that he knew the story better than she did. "What good would it do cutting the thing up?"

"Make it easier to sell."

"Four parts? You'd still recognize the picture."

"What do I know? Because they still haven't found the painting, nobody can be sure."

"Nobody knows a thing but everybody's an expert."

"At any rate they cut it. And we're going to put it back together now."

She shook the thousand pieces of the picture stolen in Palermo onto Escher's floor.

"Extraordinary. That would be the best thing, my absolute dream," she said, getting to work immediately. "Imagine finding a stolen painting. You start clearing out your attic and suddenly there's this picture that someone's hidden and partly destroyed. And it becomes your life's work to restore it. You undo the destruction!"

For a long while after that she didn't say anything else. Nellie became utterly absorbed by her work, as if this were the real painting that they had to put back together again. Reinvigorated by the talk of restoration, Escher was worried that Nellie's fine tights wouldn't survive for long on his wooden floor, which was long overdue a polish. So that they weren't bent over this puzzle for an eternity, he began with the edges—a beginner's method he usually dismissed. Nellie made good progress with the head and praying hands of St. Francis, ignoring Escher's advice that the simplest thing would be to continue with the angel's banner, as the Latin letters GLORIA IN ECCELSIS DEO were easy to place. Instead, she worked on the bowed head of the mother of God as Escher did the banner himself.

He was surprised by how quickly Nellie finished St. Francis. "Even though he wasn't alive then," she said, laughing. The outstretched arm of the angel pointing down at the newborn redeemer and his mother was also taking shape. Around midnight all that was missing of the Madonna's face was the point of her chin. Her bare right shoulder and left hand were complete too. Nellie then focused on the back of Joseph's head.

They finished at seven in the morning, and to Escher's surprise, Nellie said goodbye with a warm hug.

"Thanks!" she said. "That was lovely, Escher. I badly need a bit of sleep now. I hope I dream of the picture."

It was only after she'd left that Escher realized how knackered he was. His body must have consisted of at least a thousand parts because he could feel every single one of them. How he'd love his first cigarette in seventeen years! He went to bed, but with little hope of falling asleep. Maybe it would help if he read a few pages.

Marko, Gabi, and Ala Steiner soon settled into the new city. After just a week Gabi started in the complaints department of a bank, which the staff had dubbed "the out of office." Marko found work as an auto electrician.

He didn't mind the heat and he found people's unfriendliness reassuring, because in his former life you always had to fear for your life if someone was particularly friendly. A colleague advised him on who to bribe to get Ala into a good kindergarten. The key thing was to go as high up as he could, because if he bribed a low-level official, a child backed by a higher official could oust Ala from her place despite any payment. Marko got along very well in this city.

By the following year Ala had already started school, and it wasn't long before she had fully adopted the local dialect. Sometimes this made her parents laugh and they imitated their daughter's new slang. She found learning easy. Her parents were called into school only once, because she'd forged a signature. When Marko asked her in front of the headmistress how she'd done it so well, he realized that she'd properly assimilated to her new environment. She hadn't replied "Three-Card Monte," as per their mutual understanding.

"Lucky Seven," Ala said. Even the headmistress had to laugh.

Otherwise, nothing changed. They were a happy family who respectfully overlooked backgrounds, personal battlegrounds, and grounds for particular decisions.

It wasn't until Ala started middle school and her body over-whelmed her that everything changed. Suddenly she began to ask questions. Marko Steiner knew that his daughter's budding curiosity wasn't something he could fault. Not a character flaw as such. It just came with that age. Ala wanted to find out more—about life, her family, and especially her mysterious father about whom she knew next to nothing.

To begin with, her questioning was harmless. It started when her friend Selina bragged about having two more first names. From one day to the next she insisted on being called Selina Katharina Konstanze. Katharina and Konstanze were her grand-mothers. Ala was just Ala Steiner. Her friend's pride gnawed away at her. That evening she surprised Marko and Gabi with the question, "What were my grandmothers called?"

From her parents' scandalized faces you might have thought she'd just announced she was pregnant.

"What makes you ask?" Marko replied.

"Everyone at school has at least one middle name. Or several. Couldn't I take the names of my grandmothers too? If they had nice names, that is."

"You already have a middle name," her father said.

"No I don't!"

"Yes, you do!"

He didn't have to think about it for long.

"Hasn't your mother ever told you? Your middle name is Rmsystem."

"Whaaaat?"

Marko knew that she'd lose that disrespectful tone at some point. The challenging period would pass. A necessary phase. Development. Transitional stage. And he resisted the temptation to imitate her overdramatic "Whaaaat?"

"Rmsystem," he repeated seriously.

"That's not a name!" Ala protested, flaring up. "What's that meant to be—Rmsystem?"

"First name, Ala," Marko preached. "Second name, Rmsystem. AlaRmsystem."

Her mother was laughing so much she almost missed her glass when pouring from the bottle of Field Blend. This further incensed Ala.

"Whaaaat? Ala Rmsystem?"

Of course, they'd never let on that she owed her existence to a test to find out whether a car alarm system had stopped reacting to any sort of shaking. They thought it was none of their daughter's business that her first name was derived from the reason for their first encounter.

"Very funny," Ala protested, her face flushed and voice shrill. She was in an argumentative phase, and just like her patron saint, she kicked off at the slightest cause. Sometimes this would tempt her father to throw oil on the fire. "Because when you were born you screamed as loudly as an alarm," he said.

In the twinkling of an eye, together they'd ratcheted themselves up to the highest stage of escalation. A few tears of anger shot from Ala's eyes, and her parents' silent amusement only further infuriated her.

Eventually, Marko said, "Calm down—you can pick any name you like."

But it marked the beginning of a very difficult time.

The girl's curiosity kept growing. She didn't want to understand just the world, but people too. Surely her father must have family. A past. She was convinced that he had a fascinating secret and that it was up to her to get to the bottom of it. He probably thought she was still too little to understand. But she wasn't little anymore! Ala wouldn't leave him in peace, and her questions about his childhood became more and more invasive. What was it like when you were growing up? Marko tried not to lose his temper. She couldn't know how dangerous her questions were for him. And as there was nothing he hated more than lying to her, his lies got worse and worse. He just wanted the questions to stop.

To top it all, Ala then had a young teacher at school who gave his class small research assignments. The project for that semester was researching your family tree. Ala, who'd become slightly foreign to her parents because of the new accent, found the new teacher *über-cute*, the project *über-cool*, and she wasn't going to be *ditzy* or *chilled* about it, but work really hard to outdo everyone else.

As she got only evasive answers from her father, she began snooping around his things. Just as he, as a fifteen-year-old, had crept into Lino Carelli's car to switch the remote control for his garage door, Ala got hold of the small key to her father's personal drawer. Unlocking the drawer, however, turned out to be a bitter disappointment. While Lino Carelli, in his attempt to open his garage door, blew up his house and five of his family members, all Ala found were boring things she already knew about: his passport, insurance documents, the photo of her and her parents on the day she was born, and the cufflinks he'd worn at his wedding. The only unusual thing was a book.

Ala examined the cufflinks, tried one out in a buttonhole in her blouse, only to discover it was über-heavy, so she put it back in the drawer and opened the book at the page where her father had left an old ticket for the swimming pool.

Escher's telephone rang.

"So?" the voice of Nellie Wieselburger greeted him. Without giving him the chance to respond, she cut straight to the chase.

"I've done the deal."

"What deal?"

"What deal?" she parroted back, teasing him. "With the electricians, of course."

Escher was pleased that the funeral oration for the electrician was being sorted out. But he felt slightly offended that she'd completely skipped the Sunday they'd spent together. She didn't even mention their joint effort on the *Nativity*. It was as if it had never happened.

"Did you have a good sleep?" Escher said, trying to wrest a comment from her.

"Yes, sure did."

Before he could inquire further, she'd already launched into the details of the funeral. As if nothing had happened, as if he'd merely imagined it, she informed him of the time of the burial and all the relevant details.

"She's really sound, that woman," Nellie said.

"The widow?"

"No, the boss of Elektro Janko. I think she's a good line manager."

Escher didn't have the energy to get worked up over Nellie's use of "line manager." All he said was, "I hope she's happy for you to hand the job over to me."

"Sure. The boss had no problems. I told her that one of my colleagues would be in touch. All she was concerned about was that the bill went to her and not the widow. So it's a business invoice. I've already got the tax and VAT numbers. She also gave me the widow's email and phone number."

"Great," Escher said, with about as much enthusiasm as someone might have when a raw egg falls on the floor.

"I'll forward everything to you. Part of the package is that you can use my official email address for communicating with the bereaved. I'll give you the password."

"Great."

"Right, then," Nellie Wieselburger said, signaling the end of their conversation.

"Till then," Escher said.

He wanted to thank her but Nellie had already hung up. Within a minute he received a text with the password and all the information he needed. The widow's email address consisted of a meaningless abbreviation, and he felt annoyed that he hadn't asked Nellie for her full name.

To console himself for the bizarre phone call, Escher got going at once. The password was very useful. Avoiding a direct salutation, he sent an official message from Nellie's website to the widow, requesting a conversation. In such matters he was a real pro; it took him no time to strike the right tone. As he knew from experience, the more objective and down to earth you were, the better. He needed information about her husband to compose the oration. He requested a conversation with her—over the phone would be fine. If necessary, a few pieces of information by email, but a personal conversation would be best.

But the widow didn't reply. Not wanting to call her immediately, Escher wrote another email, and still there was no response. Maybe she didn't want an oration? He hadn't accounted for that possibility. The fact that the widow had declined to have a priest, as Nellie had mentioned, didn't mean that she was interested in a funeral orator. Did she perhaps mistrust her husband's suspiciously helpful employers? Did the widow maybe suspect a sly attempt by the firm to preempt any demands? Did she feel blindsided? Escher knew, of course, that there could be thousands of other explanations. People in mourning were not predictable; they briefly inhabited a plane of complete freedom.

To calm his nerves, Escher started another puzzle. But he was too unsettled to make a sensible choice. Now he found himself sitting on the floor with *The Creation of Adam*, which had caused him nothing but trouble from the day he'd gotten it. Instead of one thousand pieces, this one had only 999. When, after his first attempt, he found himself staring in disbelief at the gaping hole in the middle of the picture, he turned his entire apartment upside down. He even rifled through the recycling bin to find the bag the puzzle had been in. But the missing piece was nowhere to be found. To add insult to injury, the piece that was missing was the inch of void that Michelangelo had left between the human index finger and that of God, where presumably the spark would have leapt, if the damn company had included it in the first place. The only result of his lengthy complaint to the manufacturer was that they sent him the entire puzzle again—with the same piece missing.

From online forums he discovered that his fellow puzzle enthusiasts hadn't fared any better. But now this minute defect was irrelevant, for he could hardly find two pieces that fit together. He wasn't even able to finish the simple task of joining up all the edge bits. All he could think of was the widow's phone call. No matter how often he checked his cell, it wasn't on silent, and she hadn't rung. As he wasn't getting anywhere with the puzzle, he gave up and tried to read a few pages of the book.

Ala's heart stopped in horror when the bedroom door opened. She was sitting on the floor with the book, and the figure of her father, for once threatening, towered over her. But it wasn't just his imposing physical presence that frightened her, it was the quivering rage in his voice.

"What are you doing?"

"Noidea—reading," she said, presenting the book by way of proof.

"Where did you find that?"

"There?"

"What were you looking for?"

"Nothing! I was just erm . . . noidea . . . looking around!"

Ever since his daughter had been convinced that she had an idea about everything, she'd been slipping at least one mindless *noidea* into each of her utterances.

"Those are my things!" he bellowed. "You shouldn't be snooping around!"

He tried to snatch the book but his daughter was nimble and easily dodged him, shooting out the door before he could as much as curse "You little tyke!"—an expression he'd picked up during his first week of work when a colleague injured a finger on a particularly shoddy installation.

Ala walled herself up in her room, put her headphones on, cranked up the volume, and kept reading.

Three days before the funeral the widow finally called. Yes, she'd been notified by her husband's boss. Yes, yes, she was happy to have the oration. She sounded as if she'd taken a Valium. He should ask his questions now while she was on the phone. There wasn't anything interesting she could say about her husband. They were perfectly normal people. Work, family, holidays, nothing out of the ordinary.

"Was there anything your husband particularly loved?" Escher asked.

"Yes, of course," the woman said, swallowing back a tear. "Our daughter. He was a good father. He was like a father should be. Do you understand?"

"How old is your daughter?"

"Fourteen," the widow said. "She turned fourteen a month ago."

It went quiet.

Uiiiidh.

Escher broke the silence: "I'm only asking so I can get to know your husband a little for the oration. By all means tell me if any of my questions are indiscreet."

"Fire away."

"I'd be interested to know how you met your husband, if that's not—"

"He repaired my car."

"What was broken? He's an electrician!"

"That seems besides the point now, doesn't it?"

"Yes, sure, but—"

"The alarm system," the widow answered.

Uiiiiidh.

"The alarm system," Escher repeated.

"Yes, he removed the alarm."

Escher felt a cold wind blowing through his brain. He wanted a sedative now too. What was this woman saying? The widow. *Uiiidh.* The void. The absence.

"Nobody else would take it out because it's such a pain in the ass. He didn't want to either at first. But then he did. I persuaded him. And he didn't swear once. I liked that. My father swore all the time. He was full of wrath. Do you know what wrath is?"

"What do you mean?" Escher said to avoid revealing the total emptiness in his brain.

"Wrath," she said.

"Well, yes. Wrath."

"Wrath is something terrible," she said serenely. "It gets inside people. Like puppets. It's terrifying. But my husband never swore. He wasn't violent. He was a gentle man. He thought about things. He looked. He always spent a long time looking."

Escher was surprised to hear her laugh all of a sudden. "He even whispered pet names to the car when he was shaking it."

"What pet names?"

"That's not the point! He used pet names with a car rather than cursed and screamed, do you understand? That's the point!"

"Is your father still alive?" Escher asked.

"My father?"

"Yes. Your family. Are your parents still alive. Siblings?"

"That's irrelevant," the widow barked. "My family has absolutely nothing to do with my dead husband."

"You're right, of course."

"Just say in your speech that my husband was a good husband, that's enough! He was a good man! And a good father! A good person in general!"

They said goodbye.

Escher hid his face in his hands. His fingers covered his eyes and his thumbs plugged his ears. He wanted to remain like that. He tried to think whether he'd ever heard the dead man's name. Surely the police officer must have mentioned it in conversation with Janko. Or the doctor. But Escher hadn't taken it in, given the circumstances. In any case, he couldn't remember it for the life of him. He wondered whether to call the firm and ask for the name.

It struck him that the widow's email address should theoretically match the initials of her name. That was assuming she was called what he hoped she wasn't. But then he thought about it. He mustn't go to pieces. It wasn't that big a coincidence. There were lots of people with those initials. And there could be two married couples who'd met while an alarm system was being removed. Two electricians. Two daughters. There were many tradesmen who whispered to unruly equipment. Called them pet names. All of this was within the realm of possibility.

To banish the nonsense from his mind he sat down and set about the oration. He knew there was no better way of clearing his mind. And the more there was to put out of his head, the better the writing went. The more you had to keep out, the greater the pressure to produce a speech.

But Escher soon realized that it wasn't working this time. His head refused to be distracted. He could take a chance and call the widow again. Maybe she would answer with her name. Or he could ask her who'd recommended the electrician for her alarm. Who were the witnesses at their wedding? What was their daughter called?

Or he could simply call the firm and ask for the dead man's name. Even if he didn't go by Elio Russo's alias, Escher would still have the nagging thought that it was possible. And if that *was* his name, then Escher had an even bigger problem on his plate. He wondered what would happen to him if the Calabrian family discovered that he, Franz Escher, was behind Elio's murder. Elio had betrayed only one side. The other side might be plotting their bloody vengeance.

His doorbell rang. A stranger was standing in front of the camera. Escher didn't buzz the door open, and he turned off the bell.

He ran into the living room and grabbed the damn book. He wanted to know how the mess continued.

PART II

ON

The fourteen-year-old girl named after an alarm system soon made up with her father. Ala was so touched by his remorse that she not only forgave him but found herself apologizing for her part. She truly meant it in the moment, but reconciliation quickly lost its shine. After his furious outburst it had become abundantly clear that he was hiding something. His reaction spoke volumes. He must have a secret.

As Ala hadn't yet reached the age where all ethical questions are pushed to the side in resignation, she kept deliberating whether she had a right to poke around in her father's life, until the right answer emerged. "One hundred percent! I have every right!" It was, after all, her story too. A birthright. Her anger at having been taken for a fool was now greater than before, and she was utterly determined to uncover the truth.

What Ala couldn't know was that the sudden and unwanted attention from her male classmates was rooted in the very heritage

(eyes from her Grandmother Gianna, figure from her Aunt Petro-
nilla) she was trying to explore. But her hair, gumption, and brash
resolve with which she was hunting down her father's ancestors—
all of these she got from her mother.

She logged on to FAMILYTREE, one of those new platforms
that made its money from the increasingly popular hobby of
genealogy research. FAMILYTREE promised to track down missing relatives or find unknown ancestors. You could chat online
with people in other countries with the same last name, and you
could enter searches, upload photos of your family, and share
information about individual family members with the whole
world.

And recently FAMILYTREE had been vaunting its revolutionary
new service. If you provided your DNA you could find relatives
with the help of FAMILYTREE's rapidly growing genetic database.
However, this service came at a high price. If need be, she would
cobble together the money, but she decided to proceed one step
at a time. She calmly reassessed the whole thing, a habit inherited
from her father.

It would be easiest to begin with photographs. Ala started
with her favorite photo of her father, one her mother had taken
only a week into their relationship. Her father sits on an ancient
bike, looking over his shoulder, and the camera captures his
shy smile. On the back of the picture her mother had written
in pencil: "Peugeot bicycle (53) clapped-out, man (25) fresh,
photographer (21) in love."

Ala scanned the photo and uploaded it. "Who knows this

man?" she wrote as a title in the designated field. And in the fine print she explained: "This is my father. He was born in 1982. He's looking to get in touch with his relatives. The country he comes from is unknown. Europe, probably."

On the FAMILYTREE platform the text would automatically translate into the language of the user who clicked on Ala's page.

For a week nothing happened. Then she got a message. Ala clicked and a window opened: "You have a new message. Upgrade to FAMILYTREEGROWFASTER so you can read it and reply."

The subscription cost €9.90 per month or €79.90 per year. Ala paid the ten euros and to recoup the money she put a green bracelet—the catch was sort of broken anyway—on her Vinted page. She was asking for fifty euros but would be prepared to sell it for thirty. Even before completing the listing, she'd already opened the message on the FAMILYTREE site. Sender: Carlotta Esposito.

Ala couldn't believe it. She read what this Italian woman had written over and over again. She contemplated calling her father at work because she found the idea of waiting until evening unbearable. Fortunately, someone immediately wanted to buy her bracelet. The purchaser even paid the full price because he was in a great hurry to find a present. This distraction made it easier for Ala to pass the time.

"Do you know a Carlotta Esposito?"

Hopping gleefully, she greeted her father with this question when he finally came home. The slap to Ala's face was shockingly violent. His wife, who witnessed it, screamed at him in disbelief.

She used a word he'd never heard her utter before. A word that sounded as if hell had opened up.

Ala said nothing at all and just stood there in shock. She was like a street fighter relishing the serious mistake their opponent had made. As if trying to provoke him to do it again. As if she were offering the other cheek. As if she were cursing him never to forget this look on his daughter's face. As if she were waiting just one more second until he felt the knife in his back. His daughter's composure frightened Marko.

Even calmer than Ala's silent poise was the voice of his wife, who said, "Get out of here or I'll call the police!"

And Marko Steiner did what his wife demanded. Without attempting to explain or gloss over what he'd just done, he left the apartment.

For the first time in his life Marko drank himself senseless. He lay on a park bench, and as the sun rose he was surprised he'd slept at all. He had a coffee at McDonald's, washed his face in the bathroom, and went to work. Nobody noticed anything unusual.

When he came home that evening, his daughter had disappeared. Gabi had rung all her friends but nobody knew where Ala was. Marko then noticed that she had stolen all the money from his cash drawer. He hated paying by card, always preaching that it left behind a paper trail. His daughter had never stolen anything before, but now she'd absconded with more than seven hundred euros. She hadn't taken anything else except the book from her father's drawer.

Marko and Gabi had no idea that their daughter had been on

the train to Naples for hours. Ala now knew how she could find out more about her father. She ignored the messages from her parents. Her father had already sent her a million apologies. But she sensed that he still wasn't telling the truth. Fathers never told you the truth.

The only person she communicated with over the course of her journey was his cousin. Carlotta Esposito. At first, Ala had doubted Carlotta's claim that the photo was of her cousin. The photographs that Carlotta sent, supposedly Marko as a child, hadn't convinced her either. There was an uncanny resemblance, but the nose wasn't right. But in one of the photos she could have sworn it was him. She'd have spotted this smile among a million similar faces. And her father's reaction to Carlotta's name was definite proof.

This was Ala's first trip by herself on a train. So far everything had gone smoothly. Ala could look grown up if she wanted to. All the same, she was pleased that she had Carlotta to message rather than being completely alone. Carlotta expressed how much she looked forward to meeting her and sent two more photos of her father as a young man. Then communication with her slowed and during the night there was nothing more. Although she was deathly tired, Ala couldn't sleep. She was too excited. And the messages kept coming from her mother.

The later it got, the more difficult she found it to ignore them. Everything reminded her of her parents. Even the book was about an electrician. Nonetheless, she kept reading to make the time pass somehow and to calm her fears.

During his second telephone conversation with the widow, Escher persuaded her to meet him.

"Why?"

"I'd like to get a better picture," Escher explained.

"A better picture," the widow repeated. "There's nothing more to get."

He waited in silence. He'd worked with so many bereaved people.

"I'm not in the mood," she said. "I can't."

"I understand. Grief can make you speechless."

He'd never worked out any specific method for dealing with the bereaved. It was just in his nature. Maybe the truth was that he felt comfortable in their presence. He slotted in, like a puzzle piece. Coexistence without ties was his world. Nellie Wieselburger wasn't altogether wrong. Being cut off was the connection. When people were content or even happy, he found it hard to get the ball rolling. The only people he got on well with were those who'd become withdrawn, cut themselves off from others.

As a funeral orator obviously it was unprofessional to fraternize with the bereaved. Distance was everything. Otherwise, you soon became a Nellie Wieselburger, throwing herself at the mourners with her empathy. A Mitzi Stiegl who confused family grief for familiarity. Escher never forgot that the bereaved were his opponents. He mustn't give them too much latitude. He had to catch them off guard. Here there was method, of course. Tricks. Moves. If an intractable relative refused to divulge any useful information, then the only thing for it was the Three-Card Monte.

"Could you put me in contact with someone, perhaps?"

"What do you mean?"

"Family members or friends who could tell me something about your late husband."

Most people reacted badly to this question. Escher had the talent of being able to wait them out. You just had to give them time. He knew what was running through the heads of the nearest and dearest at this key moment. *Who could do this in my place? Who could I foist it on? Who could tell the funeral orator something about the deceased?* As people ran through their friends and relatives in their minds they felt aggressive toward them. *What would they say? A heap of nonsense! They'd dig out trivial stories! Put the dead person in the wrong light! They'd make it about themselves!*

As with fermentation processes and cooking techniques that need time, as with proving bread dough and pickling, infusing and simmering, the slow melting of substances and the transformation of elements, here it was all about giving the bereaved sufficient time to allow their aggression toward family and friends to fully mature. Before this maturation process was complete, they often took detours. Sometimes they even gave names, only to retract them again immediately. Maybe him—no, what would he say? Maybe his sister, no, no way his sister, she's only ever . . . Perhaps her brother, actually, no, that brother has never . . . Or his son, no, he's just, he's never . . .

Sooner or later they caved.

"Well, if you insist," the widow said. "But I'm not going out. You'll have to come to me."

"When would work?"

"I'd rather get it over with as soon as possible."

She gave him the address and told him how to get there by trolley. Escher heard an unbearably loud whistling and wasn't sure whether it had come from the phone or his ear. He knew that the widow would now tell him whose bell he had to ring. She'd only answered the phone with a "Yes?" He didn't know what her name was. She had to come out with it now.

"It's Apartment 3."

"Three?"

"Yes, that's right."

Feeling as if he'd come within a hair of being struck by lightning, Escher hung up and made his way to Apartment 3. The widow lived at the other end of the city, in a neighborhood Escher hadn't visited in decades. To pass the time he took out his book on the trolley.

"What horror story are you reading?" asked the elderly woman who'd got on in Padua with a long-haired old man. Having spent hundreds of miles discussing whether the reservations for these seats were valid, they'd made themselves at home opposite Ala, loudly commenting on the places they passed through.

"Noidea, a novel," Ala said without looking up.

"You made such a sound I got a fright."

Ala shook her head. She hadn't noticed that she'd groaned briefly at the mention of Apartment 3.

"What's it about?" the old man weighed in with a patronizing smile.

His spiders' legs were so long that Ala had sat cross-legged to get out of their way.

"It's about . . . an old man."

Ala wondered why she'd bothered to answer at all. It was none of their business that she'd moaned at the mention of Apartment 3 because this widow had the same door number as her mother. She wanted to read in peace. Ala shut the book. The car was too full to change seats.

"Oh, exciting," the old man said. "It gives me hope that there are still young people who read books."

"Don't interrupt her reading," the woman exhorted.

"I'm not interrupting. If anything it was you who interrupted."

"Don't allow yourself to be interrupted."

Ala didn't allow herself to be interrupted any longer. Escher was surprised by the reversal. Not long ago the electrician had rung his bell and now he was ringing the bell of the electrician's apartment. The apartment didn't tell him much about the dead man. Apart from the fact that he'd put spotlights in the drop ceiling. These lights depressed Escher. Ceiling spotlights reminded him of people who had ceiling spotlights. In this case he got over it quickly because who's going to fault an electrician for taking his handiwork to excess?

Maybe he'd just wanted to ensure that his wife's mop of black hair, which appeared to contain only a single strand of gray, was always well-lit. Her face reminded Escher of the Egyptian women in the puzzle *Marketplace at Giza*. The name Gabi, which she'd introduced herself with, didn't suit her at all. Names like Leyla or Nuri would have better fit this beauty with the tear-stained cheeks. Besides, only older women were called Gabi, thought Escher, whose artistic incompetence made him only too sensitive to ill-suited names. But now he was embarrassed by his reaction. His surprise must have shown on his face. As if he'd spoken his thoughts out loud, she told him how she'd come by her name. She'd never disclosed it to a single person, she said. Not even her husband. But now that everything was so terrible anyway, she finally wanted to get it off her chest.

"My father wasn't a gentle man like my late husband. He came from a culture where the man . . ."

It was part of Escher's professional routine that as soon as the bereaved started talking he became a fly on the wall. He mustn't put the speaker off with a careless reaction. All the same, she didn't finish her sentence.

"It was just part of that culture," she said, aborting her attempt at explaining. "But I can't forgive him. These men were taught that you have to protect your daughters from the world by hitting them. And it wasn't just my father who was like that. My brothers were worse."

She smiled.

"But none of it was so bad. Until I was supposed to marry. At the age of fifteen. That's when it really got going. I stopped listening. I was born in Germany. I always knew both worlds, you see? I didn't want to get married."

Escher avoided her gaze and was happy that she went on talking.

"After several hospital stays I was put into witness protection. I was given refuge by a family in a different city. It was there that I took the new name Gabi."

"Was it a nice family?"

"Yes, a very good family. I didn't move out until I was eighteen."

"And you never told your husband any of this?"

"It would have been too dangerous. The police made it clear that I mustn't tell anyone—ever. Not a soul! There was too big a risk that even years later it might occur to one of my brothers to restore the family's honor. With my blood, you see? Antiquated ideas of honor and so on."

Escher swallowed.

"Well, it's all out now," Gabi said. "It feels strange. You mustn't tell anyone."

"Of course not."

"Not a soul!"

Over his career Escher had already heard many wild confessions. The more tightknit a family appeared at first glance, the deeper the schisms. But never before had someone confided in him a secret like this.

Uiidhhh.

"We'd already been married for a few years when I spotted one of my brothers in the street. I don't know if he'd followed me or just found me by chance while visiting the capital. My daughter was four at the time. I hurried home and told my husband I wanted to move."

Escher looked at himself from a distance, sitting there as if stunned into total silence. He imagined that this was only an Escher-shaped snakeskin, while the real Escher invisibly got to his feet and made off for a different world.

"He agreed without asking any questions. That's what he was like. He had no idea why I had to move. But he understood if something was important. And so we came here."

"Was that ten years ago?" Escher said, annoyed that his voice cracked.

"Yes, almost. Sometimes I think that the main reason I was with him was because he never asked questions. I couldn't have lived with another man. One who did ask questions. I mean, I couldn't tell him the truth. If you tell just one person, witness protection collapses. That's why I never had a proper relationship beforehand, you see? Just casual stuff. But with him it wasn't a problem. He was a discreet man. I love discreet people. They're quite rare. Discreet people scarcely exist anymore. Or maybe they never did. People always want to know everything."

Escher shook his head. What he knew was already far too much. He wondered whether by "casual stuff" she meant Jens. The soles of his feet were doing warm-up exercises he hadn't instructed them to, making his knees, thighs, and entire body tremble.

"Maybe he was like that because he came from Switzerland," Gabi said.

"Your husband was Swiss?" Escher asked dumbfounded, as if this were the biggest surprise of his life.

"Yes," the widow laughed. "But he wasn't really Swiss. He just said he came from Switzerland. I'm talking nonsense."

"Did he say it to sound interesting?"

"No, not to sound interesting. He just wanted to hide his real origins."

"And when did he tell you the truth?"

"Never," the widow replied. "He was as secretive as they come. That's what I liked about him."

"Weren't you curious?"

"Maybe. But first and foremost I was glad that he didn't ask questions. Secrets aren't any more interesting when you know them. At any rate I can only tell you what I know. And that isn't much."

"It's not just about facts," Escher said. Like a drowning man he clung to his professional expertise. "The facts I get in my work from the nearest and dearest are just inventions too. Not because they lie, but . . ."

The widow's expression went so blank that he felt like someone at a trade fair trying to peddle his junk. But it was the most important principle of good funeral orations. The more facts about the deceased that were packed into a speech, the less comforted the bereaved felt. Mostly the reactions would be hostile; they would chafe at the fact that a detail wasn't exactly right. Either there was something he hadn't understood or the person he'd consulted had twisted the facts, hadn't told the whole story correctly. Dates were wrong, names were mixed up, and, as far as the bereaved were concerned, the deceased was presented in a completely false light.

The know-it-all attitude of various camps among the relatives toward the facts was not, however, the real problem. Even if they were in agreement, a retelling of someone's life could not produce any consolation. In fact, those who could agree on the facts were always the most desolate of mourners. Those cold fish didn't even allow themselves the consolation of heated arguments between relatives, pointless accusations and furious offense. The problem was simply the bleakness of reality.

Of course, as a funeral orator you couldn't simply invent something. It was all about toeing the line with your words. The invisible line between the world of what had actually happened and what could have been possible. Like a climber you mustn't slip from this ridge, either to the heaven of sheer empty rhetoric or to the hell of facts of the life lived. The climber remained where they were by falling on both sides simultaneously. Escher suspected that it was on this ridge that all ideas and knowledge were at home. You mustn't distance yourself from the facts, but nor should you stick to them. It was all about staying close by without intending to.

"Anyway, I liked him the way he was," the widow said. "Why would I want to risk that and poke around?"

"I can understand that."

"What?"

"That the mystery is exciting. After all, most people don't have any secrets. And what they think pass for secrets are—"

"I felt I knew him right from the beginning," the widow said, interrupting his Wieselburgerish ingratiation. "It's the sort of thing you sense immediately. At least that's how it was for me. The way he removed the alarm system. He was a gentle man.

He was gentle. He took his time looking over everything until he fully understood the problem. Grasped it. He looked a bit stupid while he was doing this, but he wasn't stupid, he was sensitive. That's how he was. Gentle. Then he suddenly goes and slaps our daughter!"

"Al . . .," Escher started to say, trying to interrupt, but choked on his tongue.

"Violence is a deal-breaker for me. I can't even take someone raising their voice. I've got zero tolerance for it because of my past. And the first time we met I sensed that he'd never lay a hand on me. Or even shout. He was—"

"I mustn't take up any more of your time," Escher interjected like a jittery alcoholic who's unable to wait and raises his glass for a toast in the middle of a speech. He cursed himself for not having left earlier. He didn't want to know. He was afraid of what else the widow might tell him.

"He hit her hard. *Really* hard! He was in a rage! I'd never seen him like that."

"Why was he so angry?" Escher asked. It was too late to slip away now.

"No reason. People are always angry for no reason."

"And your daughter?"

"She ran away. He never saw her again."

"When was that?"

"Just a few days ago. He was so distracted. That's why he allowed something like the circuit breakers to slip past his mind."

Escher nodded. He felt sick to his stomach. Like an old man

he put a hand on the table to help himself up and offered her the other hand to say goodbye. His knees were like a marionette's but nobody was pulling the strings. He felt the panic rising.

Back home he was so worn out that he couldn't bring himself to write the oration. Although it was fully formed in his mind, he just couldn't do it. As he took the puzzle *Black Hole 3* from the shelf, he felt the speech slowly evaporate from his brain. *Black Hole 3* had often helped him in the past when he had no idea what to do. Or *Neverending Labyrinth*. Or *Self-Portrait in a Convex Mirror*. When he was at a total loss. But no sooner was *Black Hole 3* on the floor than he wanted *Neverending Labyrinth*. He emptied it out beside *Black Hole 3*, but as soon as he started he sensed at once that he wouldn't be able to get on even with *Neverending Labyrinth* that day. He stared at the scattered piles of *Black Hole 3* and *Neverending Labyrinth* as if he were seeing a puzzle for the first time in his life. What were all these oddly shaped bits? It seemed to elude him altogether that the point was to assemble a picture. His brain was playing dumb. But he couldn't ignore the matter forever. He had to know how the electrician's daughter was now. The book was within arm's reach. If he turned his head, he could see it. If he stretched, he could grab it without getting up. If he opened it, he could continue reading.

"Where are you going?" the old lady asked after Ala declined her offer of chocolate ("It's without added sugar!").

"To noidea Lamezia."

"Gosh, that's still a long way."

Ala looked out the window.

"And you've come from Vienna?"

Ala nodded.

"I could tell immediately," the woman said with a kind smile.

"Wouldn't it have been better to go via Paola?" piped up the old man.

"Noidea, I'm being picked up."

The couple gave her a concerned look.

"I'm going to see my father's family. They're picking me up."

"Oh, how nice. Is your father from there?"

"Yes, of course."

The old man checked his phone. "Lamezia—you need to transfer at Naples."

"Where are you two going?" Ala asked. Not that she was interested. She just hoped that they would get off soon, or die—either would be to her satisfaction.

"Pompeii," the woman said.

While the old man frowned, absorbed by his phone, she prattled on to her young victim about the sights of Pompeii.

"I hope you won't miss your connection in Naples," he interrupted. "We've already got a fifteen-minute delay. And that's the last train today."

"Well, I'll just have to wait. It's not so bad. My phone's charged, nothing'll go wrong."

"Spending the night at Naples station? I don't recommend it . . ."

Ala was annoyed, and when the couple offered to put her up

in their hotel for the night, all she said was, "My father's texted me. He'll pick me up in Naples if I miss the train."

"But that's a long drive for him," the old man said skeptically. Ala had sensed for some time now that this elderly couple didn't believe her. They were worried about this girl all by herself on the train. They doubted her story about having family in Italy. Ala knew she had to be careful or risk triggering the woman's maternal instincts. She'd already raved about the mother hugging her daughter in Pompeii, taken unawares by the volcano and now on display for perpetuity.

"It would be much nicer for you to stay the night at a hotel than at Naples station," she said, trying to persuade Ala.

"Safer too," the old man added.

His wife shot him a look of reproach. She must think this was a matter to be discussed between women.

"I bet your father would rather not have to drive all that way at night too," she said.

Ala shrugged. She needed to be rid of this couple as soon as possible.

"It'll be more comfortable for you as well. And in the morning you can come and look at the excavations, they're really interesting! The memory of a lifetime! And then you can go on. That would be much nicer, wouldn't it?"

Making as if she had to pop to the bathroom, Ala exited the car. She left her backpack behind; with those two nuisances it would be safe at least until Naples. All she took with her was the book. Until the conductor came she could sit in first class and read.

Between cars, however, she ran across a group of young people. They were sitting by the bathroom door, listening to music, playing cards, and drinking beer.

"Hey, I know you," a pale boy called out in German. He had dyed black hair and pimples along his hairline that suggested an unaddressed allergy to the dye. On his forearm he had a tattoo of a power strip with three outlets. Ala thought it was a bit stupid but also somewhat cool. Maybe she wouldn't have answered him otherwise.

"How do you know I speak German?" she asked when she'd got past him.

"I guessed," he said.

"And where do you know me from?"

"You passed me on the train to Naples," he narrated theatrically. "I was sitting on the floor outside the bathroom, holding a can of beer. You came up to me and I held out the can!"

Holding out his can he said in a normal voice, "Don't you remember? It was only a second ago, you can't have forgotten!"

She suppressed a smile and went on her way. All the cars were crammed and huge suitcases obstructed the aisles. After what seemed like an eternity she got to first class. No sooner had she found a seat than the guy with his smelly can of beer materialized again. "Excuse me, is this seat free?"

Without replying, she peered out the window and he sat beside her.

"I'm Elias," he introduced himself, politely offering her his hand.

"Hello," she said and briefly held his fingers so he would take his hand away.

He laughed, amused. "Why do you lot always shake hands like that?"

"What do you mean by 'you lot'?"

"And why, when someone politely introduces themselves, do you not say your name?"

"My name is Selina Katharina."

"Nice."

"What's wrong with the way we shake hands?" Ala asked.

"Well, it feels like holding something lifeless. Like a dead fish rather than four fingers!"

"Where are you lot going?"

"What do you mean by 'you lot'?"

"You and your mates back there."

He told her they were going to Pompeii. A school trip. She said she was going there too.

"With your class?"

"Are you mad? On my own, of course."

"I bet it's going to be really eerie with all those dead people," he said.

"What's eerie about that?"

"All the dead people—that's definitely spooky."

"No idea. We'll all be in the ground sooner or later."

"Sure, but not all at the same time."

"Is that what you find spooky—everyone dying at the same time?"

"Somehow, yes."

"My name's Ala, by the way," Ala said.

"Right. That's much better than Selina Katharina. My name's Elias."

"You already told me."

To break the demonstrative silence he used to emphasize the silliness of her answer, as if it were the greatest-ever failure to understand a joke, she asked, "Why did you get a PS tattoo? It's a bit random, if you ask me."

"What's a PS?"

"Don't you know? It's a power strip."

"Never heard 'PS' before. Who calls it that?"

"My father. He's an electrician. He calls it that."

"PS," Elias laughed.

"So why have you got it?"

"So I can always charge my phone."

He reached for her book. "What are you reading?"

"A book."

After Elias had read a few lines, Ala remarked, "It's a bit spooky too."

"The book? What's off about it?"

"The characters remind me of my family."

"Books always remind you of yourself."

"The husband's an electrician. And the wife has the same first name as my mother."

"What's she called?"

"Gabi."

"Gabi!" Elias laughed. "My grannie's called Gabi. That's not spooky, at most it's a coincidence. The Bible says that I'm a prophet. But I wasn't even born yet."

At that moment they both realized that the train was pulling into Naples and raced back to their car. Elias had to get off with his group. Ala packed up her backpack and informed her self-appointed guardians that she would come to their hotel. The two of them were visibly pleased.

"Where's your luggage?"

"This is it."

They rode the bus for thirty-five minutes. She couldn't see Elias among the passengers, nor any of his schoolmates. They'd probably taken another bus to some youth hostel. Ala was miffed and, taking it out on the boring old couple, made sure not to look out the window even once and just read her book.

Escher was woken by his telephone ringing. He was relieved, because in his dream he was saving Nellie Wieselburger. Her life depended on whether he was able to finish *The Origin of the World* in time. In the dream, however, the puzzle was defective, with a piece missing, as had happened to him years earlier with a different puzzle. True to life, in this dream he also wrote a letter to the manufacturer and contacted other puzzle enthusiasts, who shared the same problem. Neither in real life nor in his dream was there a solution.

Instead of being annoyed, he was happy to be delivered from this appalling stress by the telephone. It didn't surprise him that it was Nellie Wieselburger calling him at such an ungodly hour.

"How are you?" she asked.

"Terrible," Escher said. "I had a dream about a puzzle."

"Which puzzle?"

"*The Origin of the World.*"

She gave a childish laugh. "But that's positive."

"Why are you calling me?" Escher asked in irritation, for he had no desire to go into his dream any further.

"The woman called me."

"Which woman?"

"You know, the widow."

"She called *you*?"

"Yes, that's what I'm saying."

"Why?"

"Have you forgotten that the job is being handled by my firm? Or, more accurately, *was* handled."

"What do you mean, 'was handled'?"

"If you didn't keep interrupting you'd already know. She says she doesn't need an oration anymore. Because there isn't going to be a funeral."

"What? Why?"

"She's postponing it. Until her daughter's back."

"Look, I'm still half asleep," Escher said, even though he was wide awake. "I don't understand. What's up with the daughter?"

"She didn't tell me anything else. She just said her daughter had disappeared."

"Isn't she back from Italy?"

"Why Italy?"

"I thought you said Italy."

"The nonsense you talk. Wake up, will you? Or go back to sleep. You're off the job. She can't organize a funeral while her daughter's in danger."

"Why should she be in danger?"

"No idea. She didn't go into any detail. Anyway, the oration's off."

"But she'll need one at some point, won't she?"

"You know what? Why don't you sort it out with her? I mean, you used the oration as an excuse to get in touch with me, admit it." Nellie laughed.

"Very funny."

"But feel free to call me again. Whenever you feel like it. I'd be very happy to do *The Origin of the World* with you sometime."

Escher hung up and hoped that he'd be able to get back to sleep if he read a few pages of the book. Ala's night had been too short as well. She was on her own in a hotel room for the first time. She couldn't sleep. The book was just too eerie. There was something about it that wasn't right. Like looking through a pair of binoculars the wrong way round. Makes you feel giddy. She didn't want to identify with this victim. The only thing that comforted her was the idea of Elias. He wasn't a prophet, despite what the Bible said or whatever.

She checked her phone to see if Carlotta had replied to her message. Ala had written to say she'd been forced to stay the night in Pompeii because of the delay. But come morning there was still no sign of life from her father's cousin. Ala reassured herself that it was still early. Carlotta was her father's age and in all likelihood one of those hermits who was hardly ever online, checking their messages at most once a day. This was at odds, however, with the fact that she'd been on FAMILYTREE. Ala tried to make sense of Carlotta's silence. Was it possible that she was in a huff because of the delay? Ala wrote her another message, then went downstairs for breakfast.

The fuddy-duddies had promised her that if she got to breakfast on time, they'd take her along to the world-famous excavations. She'd decided to show up as late as possible. But now it occurred to her that it might be a good idea to visit the ruins. Maybe she'd bump into Elias again. Surely, he'd be there to see the dead people with his class too.

The fuddy-duddies acted as if no one had ever paid them such an honor. They even covered her admission although she had enough money herself. The old man was thrilled that he managed to book her ticket online from the breakfast table. When the confirmation came through, he beamed and said in quaint English, "That's the way the cookie crumbles."

His wife laughed as if he'd made a joke.

Ala swore to never let herself go like this. By comparison, dying young was a mercy. In the days that followed she would often remember this thought. Die young rather than become *that*. It was unsettling that she'd had this thought.

"These online tickets," the old man said. "It used to drive me crazy. I mean, I'm no digital native. But I'm getting the hang of it. I've worked at it. I've become a bit of a"—he gave Ala a mischievous smile—"*techy nerd.*"

"Normally he lets me do it when there isn't a young woman around he's trying to impress," his wife said with a wink. This was cringe! There was nothing Ala hated more than old women joking about their husbands and winking.

As she devoured her breakfast, she realized she hadn't eaten in ages.

"There's some scrambled egg over there if you fancy it," the woman said.

When Ala shook her head, the old man said, "I bet you're a vegetarian like our niece."

"Those are vegans," his wife corrected him. "Vegetarians eat eggs."

"Anyway, we've got to get going," the old man said with a nervous glance at his watch. Ala brought her book along in case the couple tried to talk to her.

On the way to the dead people she was astonished by how many living wandered the ruins. It was going to be impossible to find Elias in this teeming crowd.

"Did they teach you about Pompeii at school?" the old man asked as they spent what felt like half a year in line.

"Yes, of course," she lied.

"In history? Or art?"

"Yes," Ala repeated.

"Could have been geography too," the old man said. "Volcanic eruptions probably fall under geography."

"More likely geology," his wife suggested.

"But geology isn't a subject at school."

When they were finally in, Ala immediately gave the two talking dolls the slip. She didn't see Elias anywhere. Nor anyone from his group. Nor was there any message from Carlotta. It was pointless checking her phone every ten seconds. But she did it nonetheless. She had no other option than to kill some time and look around a bit.

Elias's prediction hadn't been wrong. It was sort of eerie. The fact that they'd all perished at the same time. An entire people went to sleep and never woke up again. Before going to sleep they were probably thinking about a new mosaic for their bathroom and then they were drowned in lava as they slept. From the volcano. Vesuvius. Vesuvio. It erupted. Before then they'd lived pampered lives. Or at least what one might consider luxurious for back then. The fuddy-duddies of the time. Nothing had been invented back then. But they did have their own stuff, mosaics, baths, and so on. And slaves. Selina Katharina's mother always went to the wellness center. As did the other mothers. Because of the masseurs. They had the hots for the masseurs. It was called therapeutic. Wellness was cringe. It was just über-icky! All the masseurs with all her friends' frustrated mothers.

The worst thing was the gawkers. Americans, French, Chinese, German. In the heat they all stank like the plague. Maybe the plague would break out here soon. On the very spot where the volcano erupted, now the plague is going to break out. Because of the human stench. What a spooky coincidence that would be. Every day the visitors outnumbered the dead. The volcano killed five thousand. Supposedly. How could they know that for sure? Ten thousand visitors a day to Pompeii, she heard the guide of one group say. Twice as many visitors as dead people! Obviously, they knew how many tickets were sold every day. But how many dead? There were no tickets for them. Not even proper burials. A mass burial. But, such things are much better known these days. Because of DNA and that sort of thing, like on FAMILYTREE. *I'm no digital native—* how ridiculous was that?

Ala stood beside petrified bodies labeled "mother and child," but how could they know this was the mother? She was thinking it could just as well have been a nanny when she spotted Elias in the distance. She called out, but only a few idiots turned around, and when she tried to follow him there were so many tourists in the way that he was immediately swallowed up by the crowd again.

Carlotta still hadn't gotten back to her, and to forget all the madness here, Ala found shelter in the shade of a public restroom and buried herself in her book. Escher didn't wake again until noon. He immediately called the widow, but she didn't answer. After an eternity on hold with the electricians, he managed to get through to the boss, but she couldn't tell him any more than what he already knew from Nellie Wieselburger. The funeral would not take place until the daughter was back.

He went to the bathroom, made a coffee, picked up his backpack, and took the trolley to the widow's place.

Uidhhh. Have an absence. Feel an emptiness. He couldn't understand what was going on here. What was happening, in fact? The picture wasn't coming together. He was lacking necessary information. He had too much information. An infinite chasm opened up beneath his feet.

He pressed the bell to Apartment 3. The widow, her face puffy from crying, opened the door.

"Didn't your boss tell you?" she said by way of a greeting.

"My boss?"

"Nellie Wieselburger, MA. I called her."

"Yes," Escher said. "That's why I'm here."

She looked at him, baffled.

"What's happened to your daughter?"

"She's gone."

"Where to?"

She shook her head.

"I'm sorry, I really can't talk right now," she said, but lingered in the doorway as if she didn't want him to go either.

Not knowing what to do, Escher just stood there awkwardly.

"Do you have children?"

"No, I don't," Escher replied. "It never happened, sadly."

He didn't really need to pretend. The widow wasn't properly listening to him anyway. Her thoughts were completely elsewhere.

"Recently she started showing an interest in our pasts. All of a sudden, she became curious. About our family backgrounds, you know?"

Escher did know. He knew only too well. But he didn't want to know. And he kept his cool.

"I expect it's her age," he said circumspectly.

"Yes, perhaps. She started poking around in our affairs. It wound my husband up. But she didn't mean any harm."

"Probably quite the opposite."

"Yes, she was just curious. But then she put his photo on

the internet. In some search engine. Where you look for your ancestors."

"FAMILYTREE?" Escher asked.

"You know it?"

He nodded.

"After the slap he gave her for that, she was off. I mean, I can understand her," the widow said.

"She couldn't know that he—"

"—that she'd never see him again."

Escher swallowed. He was glad she was bringing the conversation to an end.

"And there's not going to be any funeral until she's back," she said. She gave Escher a nod and closed the door.

For a moment he stood there, staring at the number 3 in front of his nose, then he took the stairs. By accident he went down a flight of stairs too many, and when he realized that he was in the basement rather than at the front door, he was gripped by panic. If he took another step he'd be caught in a never-ending loop and have to go down flight after flight of stairs forever, like in that puzzle he'd so often done. To arrest the panic he sat on the step and fished the book out of his backpack.

The throngs of people made Ala feel anxious. Ever more living were mingling with the dead, ever more sweaty plague candidates were standing in line for the bathrooms, and the shade, which Ala had to keep following, was now vanishing for good. She needed to flee somewhere. She wondered whether she really had read the word FAMILYTREE in the book, or whether she had sunstroke.

Maybe the plague had already taken root in her brain. Fortunately, a message from Carlotta came at that very moment.

"Where are you?"

Carlotta said that she should go to the hotel. A ride. Carlotta's brothers were already waiting there. A white Renault right outside the entrance.

The fuddy-duddies were not pleased that Ala was leaving in such a hurry. She shouldn't go before she'd seen the highlights at least. At least the highlights, they kept insisting alternately. Don't you want to see the highlights at least? She now regretted bothering to say goodbye at all. She could have just scrammed. She even shook their hands. Despite the risk of contracting the plague. And then she was gone.

"My brothers are waiting for you outside the hotel," Carlotta Esposito had written.

Ala saw them from a distance. Two guys, one über-cute, the other looking completely clueless. They greeted her with broad smiles. At least the taller one did. He had a really nice smile. The shorter one had a toothpick in his mouth, and as a result, his smile was moronic. He held open the passenger door without removing the toothpick. This meant they were letting her sit shotgun. She liked that.

"I just need to grab my bag from the hotel," she told the brothers.

With a bizarre jerk of his head the toothpick guy indicated the back seat. Her backpack was already there.

"But . . ." Ala stammered, confused. "How? It was in the hotel!"

Now he took out the toothpick, held it between thumb and middle finger, and, with his freed-up index finger, pointed at the driver. "That's Fabio. I'm Corrado."

Corrado didn't explain how they'd gotten hold of the backpack.

Probably with Lucky Seven, Ala told herself. She would have liked to have said this, but it probably didn't have the same ring for Italians. At any rate the whole thing made her a little uneasy. But if she was going to find out the truth, she had to play along as if everything were fine. She plunked herself in the passenger seat as if she were a millionaire's daughter from Malibu or a world-famous singer, Fabio her friendly driver, and Corrado her dull bodyguard. She really needed to instruct her staff to use a less noxious aftershave.

No sooner had they gotten going than Carlotta asked if everything was alright. Ala sent her a thumbs-up emoji, even though nothing was alright. The driver was getting on her nerves because he was blabbing away in truly appalling English. But she had no desire to chat. No desire and no time. She had to find out what that slap was about. She felt like slapping herself for not having gotten Elias's number. Ala would have loved to have asked him now whether he, the biblical prophet, still didn't think it was eerie. It wasn't just Apartment 3 and Gabi. There was FAMILYTREE too and the slap! Although reading made her carsick, she ignored Fabio and opened the book.

When Gabi, the widow, was taking out the trash, she found Escher on the basement stairs.

"Are you unwell?" she said, startled, and invited him up to her apartment.

Escher sat on the sofa and she poured them both a cup of tea. He turned down the offer of sugar and it struck him that he'd never drunk such strong tea in his life. Her spoon clinked as she stirred hers and began to talk.

"With her sleuthing Ala actually managed to track down his relatives. In Calabria!"

Now he took a lump of sugar after all, to stop himself from going mad on the spot.

"I mean, she had no idea that her father was in witness protection. I didn't know either. I always thought I was the only one in such cahoots. But he was too! You're not allowed to talk about it."

"And your daughter blew his cover? Did she tell you?"

"No, she didn't say a word. She just disappeared. After the slap she was gone."

"Has your daughter gone to see the relatives?"

Gabi gave a bitter laugh. "That sounds so innocent. A visit to the relatives. But these aren't normal relatives! Maybe they aren't family at all. Or perhaps everyone's related somehow in those Hicksvilles. What do I know? Anyhow, these are the people he was on the run from. In witness protection. Then he got a call. They've got our daughter. She went to see them and they kidnapped her."

"When was that?"

"The call came the evening before he died. It was our daughter on the phone. She was howling. My husband talked to her.

But then someone must've snatched the phone off her. All of a sudden, my husband was speaking in a language I'd never heard before. Not the normal Italian everyone knows. From songs or films."

"A dialect?"

"Probably. A frightful dialect. He sounded like someone after Novocain at the dentist. The next morning my husband went to work totally dejected. And he never came home."

"And you didn't know he was under witness protection?"

"Of course not! He only told me after that phone call."

"That's terrible."

"What was terrible was seeing him go to work so dejected. Didn't you notice anything?"

"Me?" Escher asked, puzzled.

"I mean, when he got to yours. Didn't you notice anything? He must have been all over the place."

"He was very quiet, but I mean, I don't know what he's like normally."

Was like, he thought, but didn't correct himself.

"Well, you couldn't have known that your electrician had just received a phone call from his daughter's abductors."

Escher found himself in an unbearable dilemma. He had killed her husband by accident and now the widow was giving him the perfect alibi. For the first time since the accident, he was close to coming clean. He wanted to confess, "It wasn't a proper accident." But maybe that wasn't top of mind for the widow, seeing as how she was consumed by fear for her daughter.

"Sometimes I think he did it on purpose," Gabi said. "To protect our daughter from the vendetta. If he's dead, they can let her go."

Escher almost laughed. Did that mean that by flipping the circuit breakers he might have saved her daughter's life?

"But that's not happened," the widow said. "They still haven't let her go."

Escher asked if he could use her bathroom. He needed a moment alone. He locked the door and sat on the edge of the bathtub. The electrician's bathroom was much nicer than his own. The tiny tiles on the walls shimmered magically. There was a proper terrazzo floor. *Surely, she had always known her husband was Italian*, Escher thought, annoyed. Although he hadn't used the toilet, he flushed and washed his hands. He tried not to catch his face in the electrician's bathroom mirror, and it struck him that his hands looked like those in *Pilate Washing His Hands in Innocence.*

"Are you saying that if it weren't for that phone call you never would have known your husband was in witness protection?" he asked as he returned to the living room.

"Yes, we were up all night and he told me everything. About all the Lucianos and Tonis and Ginos. My head was spinning," the widow laughed. "But I can't tell you all about it now. I'm so tired."

Escher was glad that the widow was asking him to leave her in peace. Before he went, he posed one final question: "Did you tell him that you actually had a different name?"

"No," the widow said. "I wanted to. But it was all too much for one night. I put it off till the next day. But there was no next day."

Escher went home as quickly as he could, to find out from the book what then happened with all the Lucianos and Tonis and Ginos.

Ala was feeling carsick from reading and asked Fabio to stop briefly. He pretended not to hear, but Corrado handed her a water bottle from the back seat. She complained to Carlotta that the two men wouldn't let her out, and Carlotta replied a second later. She shouldn't take it the wrong way—they were almost there.

"*Arriviamo subito.*"

Ala understood *subito* and calmed down. She didn't wonder why the answer was in Italian. Something she would beat herself up for later. It didn't occur to her that it was Corrado getting her messages in the back seat and replying. How could she be so stupid? It never crossed her mind that the water she had drunk was the reason for the sudden fatigue that had come over her. The music got slower and slower. One tunnel followed the next. She was amazed by the pattern produced by the lights. She wondered—

When they arrived, she didn't have a clue how long she'd been asleep. She had no sense of time because they'd taken her phone. Corrado grabbed her so roughly by the arm that she yelped. He took her into the ugliest prefabricated building she'd ever seen. The elevator stank of cigarette smoke and piss. It was graffitied from top to bottom. Vulgar images, names, and incomprehensible words. With a rattle, a rumble, and a loud bang the elevator started rising. Ala was anxious that it might stop. Or plummet. Still, the lift crashing to the ground was preferable to being stuck in here with Corrado. Right at the top the elevator stopped with a jolt, as if it had actually plummeted. Corrado dragged her out, unlocked one of the doors, and threw her into an apartment.

It was this same rundown hovel with windows screwed shut that she was now sitting in. "Now" was three days later. Or four. She'd slept a few times anyway and had woken up a few times. But she fell asleep during the daytime too and lay awake at night. Sometimes they brought her something to eat. And bottles of water. If she crushed them with her foot, they made a noise. If she threw them against the wall, no one responded. Maybe it had been three weeks. Noidea.

She only knew dumps like this from films. Junkies lived like this. Outside she could see abandoned tower blocks, warehouses, and the motorway. She wished the motorway bridge would collapse like she'd seen on television once, but the cars just kept driving. So what? She stopped looking outside. Ala spent her days staring at the ceiling. She wanted to die because she'd betrayed her father. Now she realized that he'd had very good reasons to keep his past a secret. And she was the dumb bitch who'd screwed it all up. If she screamed her head off, nobody reacted. Could anybody hear her at all? What did these people want from her? What time was it? What day of the week? What date?

How could she figure this out without a phone? At least they'd left her the book. To begin with, she hadn't been able to understand anything in it, but you could keep reading the same sentence. You could keep reading the same sentence. Then she did get into the plot and read on. There was something intriguing about the funeral orations. As if that Escher had written them specifically for her. You became so drawn in by his speeches that you got the impression the deceased still had a promising life ahead of them. He could turn time around. For Escher it only began with the funeral. Spooky.

Ala was not surprised that he was having real trouble with his current speech. He was to blame for the man's death. But he couldn't talk about that. And now, to top it all, his doorbell rang. He'd forgotten to switch it off. Although he loved the mute button, the doorbell was on. He went to the intercom and saw Nellie Wieselburger's head on the screen. She'd turned up at his door unannounced. Escher couldn't decide whether or not to let her in.

"Open up!" her eyes said as she craned her neck to the camera. Even in the video feed it was hard to evade those eyes. Maybe it was because they were so far apart that Escher's brain now got its wires crossed. Refusing to comply with his decision, his fingers rebelled, pressing the blue door opener rather than the mute button. To save face Escher didn't say a "Hello" into the intercom. No word of acknowledgment, let alone a greeting. It would have been a bit weird if, after having ignored her calls all this time, he'd started talking to her via the intercom.

In any case she was standing before him a few seconds later. When Nellie Wieselburger came rushing, the elevator wasn't going to make her wait.

"Sorry to drop in on you like this," she said by way of a greeting, "but you never answer your phone."

"When I'm working I always put it on silent," Escher said. "And then I forget to switch it on again."

"Whatever. I just wanted to return your St. John," she said, handing him the box.

"You didn't need to hurry back with it."

Escher was proud of this subtle jab. It'd just popped into his head. There was, in fact, something rather sudden about the return of the puzzle after she'd held the decapitated Baptist captive for more than twenty years.

"Maybe it's gained some interest and now there are 1,100 pieces," she joked. "You'll have to count."

"*Jokey Words in the Hallway*," Escher said, trying in vain to outdo her. "There could be a painting with a title like that."

"If so it could only be by Dix."

"Deix?"

"Manfred Deix? No, Dix! Otto Dix!"

"I see. Well, come on in, then."

"Sorry, I've got to run."

"Oh, a little coffee couldn't hurt, could it?"

She rolled her eyes and made a theatrical gesture with her hands, as if she still hadn't come down from the hysterical title *Jokey Words in the Hallway*.

"I almost didn't recognize you on the security camera."

"You were watching me on the security camera?"

"Not watching. But people look so compressed in the camera.

Maybe you could include that in your dissertation. To broaden the topic. The Cut and the Compressed."

"The compressed," she said scornfully. "But that's to do with perspective and I'm not in the sligh—"

She bent down to take off her boots, which were so tight that Escher was amazed she'd gotten into them.

"—test bit interested in perspective. Cut is the opposite of perspective. Perspective is a trick! And cut is genuine!"

Over coffee in his small kitchen he tried again to persuade her that without the compressed, her dissertation was only half of one, but she just let him talk and when he wouldn't stop she put an end to the conversation with a single word.

"Escher," she said.

That was all. Only "Escher." Without any particular emphasis, which meant something like: Escher, you can talk the hind legs off a donkey.

To help him back to his feet after this crushing blow she proposed a new topic: "Do you know what? I actually did your *Beheading* once."

"My beheading?"

"You know, your St. John. And do you know what? It occurred to me that the beheading isn't about cutting the head off. It's about putting it together."

"What else would you do with a puzzle?"

"I'm not talking about the puzzle! Don't you understand? Decapitation is about assembly. You can just as easily view the images the other way around, as if they're not cutting the head off, but attaching it! It's like inverting death, do you get me?"

"Interesting," Escher said, in the sense of, interesting that you find something so uninteresting interesting.

"Yes, really interesting!" Nellie gave a desperate laugh. "That's why I changed the subject! I've got your *Beheading* to thank for that. You sense that you can put the head back on, do you get me?"

He didn't understand why she explained everything to him twice, but just nodded with a head that was still attached to his neck and let her continue.

"Like a transplant! And do you know why John the Baptist of all people was beheaded?"

"Sure, because of Herod's wife."

"Oh that's just childish crap. Because of Christianity! Because the entire belief system separated the head from the body, Escher! That's my thesis. The Nellie Wieselburger thesis. Christianity separated the head from the body, just savor that slowly. Everybody knows this, of course, but I only became properly aware of it thanks to your shitty puzzle. And the painters are trying to put it back on. They're restoring the contact between the head and the body—like an electrician!"

"Like an electrician!" Escher repeated, shocked.

"Yes, it suddenly dawned on me! It's like a film playing in reverse if you put together a beheading with a puzzle."

"Anyway, it's great if you can work an idea like that into your dissertation," Escher said, turning to the puzzle shelf. He was already looking forward to embarking on a new one once the hysterical Nellie was finally gone.

"You should embark on something new," Nellie said. "Or do you intend just to . . ."

She stopped mid-sentence.

"Look over that way again."

"Why?"

"Just do it. Turn your whole body to the side."

Nellie reached out and caressed his brow.

"Now put your head back. Stay like that!"

She got up and looked at him from every angle.

"What are you doing?"

"Wait. Almost done."

She took her phone out of her handbag.

"Turn around, no, not like that. With your back to the table. And rest the back of your head on the tabletop. Yes, just like that. Imagine you've gone to the barber's and you're getting your hair washed."

She leaped to her feet, tipped out the rotten bananas from Escher's silver fruit bowl, and pushed it beneath his head.

"Extraordinary. Don't move!"

She turned the water on and dampened the locks of his hair, which, weighed down, hung from his head into the silver bowl.

"It's uncanny," Nellie said, taking a few snaps with her phone. "Have you ever noticed just how much you look like the head of St. John by Giovan Francesco Maineri?"

"Very funny," Escher said, sitting up testily.

"Yes, really," she said and gave Escher a bloody neck with the drawing tools on her photo app. "I always knew you reminded me of someone!" she announced gleefully, showing him first the edited image of him, then the painting that consisted only of the decapitated head in a silver bowl. "And now I've seen it. That's you!"

"You're off your rocker," Escher said, trying to hide the fact that he felt flattered.

"Don't you have the painting in puzzle form?"

"Do you think I've got every painting?"

"You mean you've got everything but this one?" Nellie said sulkily, as if she didn't believe him. She sent him the photo.

Then she restyled his wet hair because she couldn't get enough of his uncanny resemblance to the decapitee. The water ran down his neck, but as her fingers felt so nice on his scalp he didn't immediately protest. But just as he'd gotten used to the water behind him and warmed to the thought that she might keep on caressing him with her hand, she stopped and said goodbye.

When the madwoman was gone, he fetched the puzzle from the shelf. He'd lied. Of course he had Maineri's *Head of St. John the Baptist*. Escher stared at the picture. He'd never noticed the resemblance, but Nellie wasn't entirely wrong. All the same, he had decided to cut her off. He just found her too wacky. Not even the most gorgeous neck and softest fingers in the world could make up for that.

He really felt like putting together his decapitated doppelgänger, but he knew that there was something more pressing at hand. All that he retained from Nellie's impromptu visit was her flippant reference to the "electrician." He was worried about Ala. The book was still there, and because nobody had as of yet beheaded him, Escher had to go on reading.

Normally, when Corrado brought her food, he didn't knock,

but he didn't come into the room either. Like a caveman he would thrash some unlovely object against the door as if he'd forgotten each time that you needed a key to unlock it. And a second later he was in the room.

Ala noticed that he became nervous when she didn't eat anything. Perhaps that was a good sign. He even tried to be encouraging. She only had to stick this out for a few more days, he said. Soon she'd be free.

"You stink," Ala said without looking at him.

"Eat! Or you'll be dead by the time the money gets here."

"How much?" Ala said.

"Three million."

"We don't have that kind of money," Ala said.

Even though she left her food untouched, Corrado made sure to come with a new bowl every day and took the old one away. His aunt Madrisa had made the food specially for her, he claimed. She was offended when Ala didn't eat.

Ala didn't answer. She ignored the new food he had brought and waited patiently until he'd left with the full bowl from the previous day. The less she ate, the less likely she was to read the book. Because in that book there were things she didn't want to know. She couldn't care less about that Escher and that Wiesel-burger. But she didn't want to know anything about the dead electrician either, and if she ate nothing, soon she wouldn't be up to reading anything. The letters were already swimming before her eyes. But if she drank a few mouthfuls of water and stared at the page for long enough, they came back into focus.

At that very moment Escher was disturbed from his reading by the brutal chime of his phone.

"You'll have to excuse me for waylaying you with my entire story," the widow said.

"Oh, but you don't have to—"

"I'm just churning, really badly. I need someone to talk to about it."

"You can tell me everything. Nobody will hear a peep from me."

"I'm scared to talk over the phone. Could we perhaps meet?"

"Sure."

"You mustn't talk to a single person about it!" the widow snapped.

"Of course not. I'll head over now, if that's okay."

Leaping straight into a taxi turned out to be a mistake. He ought to have given the widow more time. She was in such a state that he quickly forgot to take out the two pastries he'd bought at the bakery beside the taxi stand. She offered him a cup of tea but then took half an hour to make it. Carried away by her tale, she didn't notice the water had boiled, letting it cool again in the kettle. Holding the tea strainer she said to him, "When I got the news about my husband's death I briefly thought that maybe you—"

"What did you think?"

"I'm sorry. Don't take it personally. I know it's not true. But the accident happened right after their phone call. Well, the day afterward. And so, I briefly thought that you—"

"That I what?"

"That you were one of them."

"One of who?"

"You know—"

"The Mafia?" Escher asked, bewildered. "Did you think I'd killed him?"

"On their orders."

"Me?"

"Because of the vendetta."

"I really don't know what to say."

"Yes, my apologies. It was just a fleeting thought. In shock. To be honest it was even a hope. I thought that if his relatives had killed him, they'd let our daughter go free. Because at least in their sick minds they'd have had their revenge."

"I understand."

"You don't understand anything," the widow said. "And nor do I. Because they're not releasing our daughter. Even though my husband is dead."

"Maybe they've no idea your husband's dead."

"Of course they do! They called!" she said, crossly.

"They rang you?"

"Of course," the widow said with the bitter haughtiness of someone who's privy to a catastrophe.

"And you're telling me they're still not satisfied? Even though your husband's dead?"

"They don't stick to any sort of rules. They're even asking for money for her release."

"How much?"

Escher wanted it to be any sum, just not three million.

The widow gave an acerbic laugh. "Too much."

"How about going to the police?"

"Then my daughter's dead."

Escher kept a straight face as she told him what he already knew. That Ala was locked up in an abandoned tower block. That she wasn't touching her food and was starving herself. That the ransom demand was impossibly high.

Escher didn't say three million. He didn't say anything. He let the widow talk. Maybe it was doing her good.

She'd told the kidnapper that her husband was dead so there was no reason to keep the blood feud going any longer. But he claimed it was no longer personal; the score was settled. It was just a matter of business now. Searching for the traitor had cost them a lot of dough over the past two decades. Now they wanted their expenses reimbursed.

"Expenses! They're demanding expenses for the release of our daughter!"

"How much?" Escher asked, in the childish hope that she might actually say a different amount. Any old number.

"Why do you want to know?" the widow asked. "Nobody's got three million euros to spare."

As if both his legs had gone to sleep from one second to the next, Escher felt the ground disappear beneath his feet.

"Three million," the widow said, now aping Corrado's English accent. "He's not saying anything else."

Escher cleared his throat.

"Maybe you could do a crowdfunder," Escher suggested, scraping away at the parquet with his feet like a madman, in an attempt to gain some purchase.

"A crowdfunder," the woman repeated in horror. "Do you honestly think you can set up something like that without the police getting wind?"

Although he didn't believe in it himself, Escher was annoyed that she was pooh-poohing his idea. Then they sat for a while in silence. The silence did them some good.

"Now I haven't even made the tea!" the widow realized to her dismay.

Fortunately, she didn't insist on brewing another pot, allowing Escher to say a hurried goodbye and clear off.

He walked the whole way, scarfing down both the cakes as he went. His brain was greedy for sugar and was looking for a way of raising the money. It was his chance to mitigate his guilt for the electrician's death. At the very least he was eager to make a contribution to the ransom money. Although he didn't have any savings, he didn't need the paltry nest egg that might be left from his pension plan shares. He wasn't planning to grow terribly old anyway. The most difficult funeral orations were always for those who'd been ancient, because their children were already too old to play the part of the bereaved.

Once home he immediately called the bank to find out what he'd get for the old shares. But he was merely put on hold. If you want this, press one; if you want that, press two. If you want something else, press three.

"If you want to shoot yourself, press the trigger," he muttered, pressing one of the buttons.

And so, he went from one line to another, never getting through to a human being. The music didn't even change as he moved from one level of the game to the next. Turning the volume of his mobile so low that he only just heard it, he allowed the interminable hold to keep going while he tried to get back into his book.

Ala wondered where Corrado was. Had he given up because she wasn't touching any of her food? Another possibility was that a day hadn't yet passed since his last visit. She'd probably just nodded off while reading. Why else would her face be up against the page and a few huge letters right in front of her eyes? Although the letters were reversed in this position, it didn't change the meaning: alA.

Alarmed by the different noises coming from his phone, Escher gave a start. A woman's voice announced herself politely and asked how she could be of assistance.

"I don't believe it!" Escher said in an exaggeratedly cheerful voice, to prevent himself from venting his frustration at the unknown woman.

"Have you been waiting long?"

"I've read two books in the meantime," Escher joked.

"I'm sorry for the wait."

The woman was so friendly that Escher wondered whether she might not be an AI. Preferring to believe that she was human, he said placatingly, "We have such a wrong conception about time. Our conception is too linear. We think it goes in one direction. But really you need to think of it as a loop."

"Well, maybe I can recoup some time for you," the representative said, merrily parading her incomprehension. Coupled with her bold friendliness, it was strong evidence, Escher thought, that this indeed was a fellow human. "What can I do for you today, Herr Escher?"

The telephone number must have been assigned to his account.

"Many years ago I bought some shares," he explained, wondering whether there might not be a more professional way of saying this. "I'd be interested to know if they're worth anything now. They completely crashed after I bought them. But maybe they've recovered a bit in the meantime."

"You can very easily access that information online through your banking account," the friendly woman explained.

"Not in my case," Escher said. "The shares and their owner predate online banking. They come from a time"—he paused theatrically—"when banking was still carried out in branches and on paper."

"I see," the woman said doubtfully. "Well, perhaps you could give me your account number and password."

Escher wondered how she knew his name if she was asking for his account number.

"I'm afraid I've forgotten the password. It's more than twenty years ago."

"Oh, that's too bad." She laughed. "You've got a really choice password."

"I've no idea."

"Maybe I can help jog your memory. It's got something to do with painting."

"Painting?"

Escher's mind went completely blank. There was no way the password could still be anywhere in his brain.

"Erm, how should I put it?" the woman said. "Today people take selfies. But in the past, a painter . . ."

"Self-portrait?"

"Yes, very good! That's the first part. There's a bit more to it."

"*Self-Portrait in a Convex Mirror.*"

"Well, well, what can I say? I'd love to have your memory," she chirped joyfully. "That really is an unusual password, Herr Escher."

He heard her begin to tap away frantically at the keyboard. Maybe it was a bad connection. Or perhaps she'd just muted him and he was hearing the line or the universe crackle.

"Are you still there?" Escher said.

"Yes, yes. Please bear with me, Herr Escher."

She no longer sounded so polite, more monosyllabic.

"Tell me your address again, Herr Escher."

Escher wondered what information they had and what they didn't. Was she verifying his identity or was she having to put on a data-privacy show? To get back for the performance he was being subjected to, he spelled out the name of his street with deliberate pedantry:

Romeo

Echo

Bravo

Hotel

Alpha

November

November

Golf

Alpha

Sierra

Sierra

Echo

"Now we've got two N's."

"Yes, it's written with two N's. Maybe it's a proper name."

"And without the H."

"With an H."

"And what's your date of birth?"

Escher told her everything she wanted to know.

"I've got a different phone number down here," she said suspiciously. "For a landline."

"Yes, landlines still existed in those days."

She thought about it for a moment, then said, "I can't process your question here."

"Process?"

"I'm afraid you'll have to pop into a physical branch. If you like, I could schedule you an appointment with an advisor for tomorrow."

"I'd prefer today."

"Today? I fear—"

She put the hold music on, and just as he thought she'd booted him off the call, she was back. She'd managed to get him an appointment for that afternoon.

"And be sure to bring your ID card."

"Will a driver's license do?"

"Your ID card would be best. Or passport. Driver's licenses are always tricky. Is there anything else I can help you with today?"

Escher said a friendly goodbye. He was happy that the appointment time would give him sufficient time to read some more.

The last food Corrado had brought Ala was beginning to go moldy and smell. Had he stopped coming because she'd ignored his dishes once too often? Or had he simply forgotten her?

Or was he sick?

Or had somebody shot him and nobody knew where he was?

Or had they not received their money?

Or had they received their money and were now just letting Ala rot here because it was too much effort or too dangerous to let her go? After all, she'd seen his face. Ala knew in films that it was always a bad sign if abductors showed themselves to their hostages. She'd seen the driver too.

The advantage of starving yourself was that you didn't care about much. Even the fear inside you starved.

She removed the aluminum foil from the porcelain bowl and inspected the mold. It looked very beautiful. Much more beautiful than the view she got when she looked out of the window. The sight of the rotten food brought tears to Ala's eyes. Wasting food was bad manners. So she dipped her hand in and smeared the moldy stuff on the windowpanes. The wasted food was good for something. With the serious focus of an artist she coated the glass. Now it was much nicer in here. It gave her apartment that certain something. Ala couldn't understand why this idea hadn't occurred to her before. She coated the bathroom mirror too, but because she couldn't cover it completely she threw the empty bowl at it and was surprised by how easily it shattered.

Ala had to resist the temptation to continue reading the book. She didn't want to find out how the story went on. To be on the safe side, she tore out the unread pages to flush them down the toilet. But even holding the pages was a mistake.

Escher entered the bank where he had his appointment. With a pointing finger the woman at reception indicated a desk where a very thin woman, whose hairclip perched on the back of her head like a huge spider, was staring at a screen. Escher did not exclude the possibility that the spider was forcing her to sit there and get on with her work.

"How may I help you today, Herr Escher?" she asked earnestly, her eyes still fixed on the computer screen, where she was carrying out another task. Escher's eyes deciphered the letters on her name badge, which looked far too heavy for the fine material of her business jacket: Karoline Nechvatal. For Escher, having a name badge was the worst thing that could happen to you in life. Only when Frau Nechvatal looked at him did he say to her exactly what he'd told the woman on the phone three hours earlier. He showed her his passport and the thirty-year-old scrap of paper he'd been given for his shares back at the time. She glanced at it, then typed something into her computer.

"Riiiiight," Karoline Nechvatal said, clicking her mouse, typing, clicking again, then turning to her customer.

"And what precisely would you like to do with your securities?" the bank clerk said.

"I'd just like to know roughly how much they're worth."

"Riiiiight," Frau Nechvatal said, typing and clicking in various movements. Escher got the impression she didn't know what she was doing. Maybe they'd switched systems and she hadn't totally gotten the hang of it yet. Maybe she had problems in general keeping up with the rapid pace of change. Escher would have understood that. He'd also lost the desire for updates, apps, and PINs. He'd love to be able to donate to a terrorist organization that destroyed the internet, but, tragically, to find the right people you'd probably need to know your way around the internet.

"Riiiiight, almost there. Through digitization . . ." she said, launching into an explanation, but failing to finish her sentence, merely raising her eyebrows and typing more.

Finally, she tore her gaze away from the screen and looked Escher in the eye, as if he were a bank robber who'd slipped her a note saying, "Keep smiling and hand over the cash."

"I'm going to have to fetch a colleague who handles these matters," she said eventually, then pushed her swivel chair back and tottered off, saying, "He'll process this for you straightaway."

She clattered on her heels through a discreet door that Escher hadn't noticed before. Someone had told him that bank employees got a clothing stipend. Were there vouchers for certain shops and that's why they all looked the same?

After a while she returned with a very tall man in an ill-fitting suit. He probably didn't find it easy to get things in his size. Or maybe it was just the awkward way his bony body moved that made the suit look so big. With every step he seemed to be expressing his indignation that every room, door, and piece of furniture was too small for him. Next to him Frau Nechvatal looked as elegant as a ballet dancer. Because of their contrasting footwear and builds, the way the two of them moved was strikingly dissimilar. A comical pairing. In a cartoon, they would be two animals that didn't go together at all. But Escher couldn't decide which animals they actually resembled. Despite their fundamental differences they approached Escher at exactly the same speed. It looked to him like an exercise for physics students. He was certain you could digitize both skeletons and then, with the help of a geometric movement analysis, calculate how these completely different levers, forces, and curves could result in exactly the same velocity.

The bank advisor clasped a transparent folder containing a few printouts. Fixed to his jacket was a badge identifying him as Herr Nagy.

"Herr Escher, could I ask you to come into my office please?" Herr Nagy said, stooping down to appear less imposing. "I'm afraid we're going to have to go to the building next door. That's where our private banking department is."

"It has its own wing?" Escher asked in disbelief.

"Its own building," chuckled the man, whose gentle irony

struck Escher as congenial. Maybe this was the usual temperament of people too tall for everything, he thought.

Escher followed him to the elevator. On the fourth floor they crossed a glass skyway to the neighboring building, where they were welcomed by a beaming receptionist. Herr Nagy asked whether the Zurich meeting room was free. The receptionist checked her screen and replied that regrettably it was not. Paris was free, or Tokyo.

Herr Nagy's expression darkened. "Tokyo, then," he said huffily. "Paris is right above a construction site. You can't hear yourself think, let alone have a meaningful consultation."

"Yes, it's still loud," she said, in the tone of a comforting kindergarten teacher. "Okey-dokey, I'll book Tokyo for you, then."

Ignoring her, the bank advisor turned to Escher to make it clear with raised eyebrows that his annoyance was not in the slightest directed at him, their highly valued client, but toward the circumstances. Indeed he, the firm's representative for Escher, the client, had even expressed irritation toward his employer on account of the inadequate state of the institution's premises.

The oval conference table in Tokyo gave rise to an awkward seating arrangement. Escher had often wondered why there was no proper word in German for *awkward*. How could such a critical situation have no word in a language?

"May I ask you when you last checked your portfolio?" Herr Nagy inquired when they were sitting at the conference table in Tokyo.

"Never. Back then I just wanted to get rid of the money, you see?"

The bank advisor shook his head in astonishment. He stared at the piece of paper his colleague had printed out for him. Maybe here in the private banking department it was seen as more polite not to use a computer. Escher liked the sound of that.

"At the time I had ten thousand marks I didn't need," he explained.

"Marks?"

"Seventy thousand schillings. I'm only saying marks because I got the money from Germany. A mark was worth seven schillings at the time."

"Ten thousand marks."

"Yes," Escher laughed. "These days it sounds like 'old francs.'"

As if it were up to him to console the increasingly pale-looking bank advisor, he added, "It's not so awful if the money's gone. I don't absolutely need it."

Herr Nagy laid the pieces of paper on the desk, ran an eye over them again, and launched into his prepared speech: "In 1996, that is, before the introduction of the euro, you purchased your shares at a value of approximately seventy thousand schillings. In the currency of the time, that corresponded roughly to the ten thousand marks you mentioned. At a rough estimate that's about five thousand euros in today's money. Which is irrelevant anyway as the price was calculated in dollars."

Escher nodded. He wondered why people always started off by telling you the things you already knew. To speed things up he told the ashen-faced man, "Yes, I bought shares in a book retailer.

I'd earned the money from my flop of a book. It was released by a German publishing house, hence the marks. I spent three years writing it and I was paid ten thousand marks. That comes out to, so to speak, an annual salary of three thousand marks, twenty thousand schillings! Or, fifteen hundred euros! For each year's work!"

"Three thousand three hundred marks," the man said, nodding with his calculator. "Recurring. That wasn't much at the time."

"And so I came to the conclusion that I had to buy into the capitalist system."

The bank advisor laughed with his lips shut, as if Escher had used an improper word or cracked a daring insider joke.

"As they say, it's better to found a bank than rob one."

"Yes," Herr Nagy chuckled. "We like to quote Brecht around here too. Also robbing banks is not at all advisable. Leave that to the desperate. Everything has just become too secure: we don't hold cash in the branches anymore. But founding a bank is nothing to write home about either, if I'm allowed to spill the beans."

"Bookstores went the way of the dinosaurs. The electronic world began its triumphant march and books fell out of demand. Newspapers have since bitten the dust too."

"Bitten the dust, yes," the bank advisor said, smiling. "I haven't heard that expression in a while. Even though here we often deal with firms that bite the dust."

"It's easy to slip up," Escher said. "I'm the best example of that. No sooner had I bought the shares than they were at rock bottom. In fact, they were even below the rocks. Now whenever anybody says the word 'bookstore' to me, all I hear is 'blunder.'"

"There was a dramatic fall in the share price," the advisor

confirmed, showing him the curve among his documents. "But it was just a short-term loss of confidence by investors. The recovery came really quickly. In the long term your bookstore didn't go downhill at all. Over the years your shares have risen to the value of three million euros. So your blunder unearthed a gold mine below the rocks, so to speak."

Escher didn't react. He couldn't understand what this bank advisor was getting at with this irony in the Tokyo meeting room.

"That was a very smart investment on your part," Herr Nagy said approvingly. "You recognized the potential of this stock early on. At the time nobody believed that the future of bookstores might be online. Paper and screens—they didn't go together. I remember people telling me about the imminent collapse of that chimera. In fact, I had a few of those risky shares in my own portfolio. But I sold them just in time," he joked sourly. "I told myself I'd gotten off lightly with a 20 percent loss. Of course, it was stupid of me. Really stupid. In retrospect, the most foolish thing I've ever done. You were much smarter. In the meantime, your investment has . . ."—he typed something into his calculator with his long, thin fingers—". . . pretty much risen six hundredfold. Over thirty years that's an annual interest rate of 20 percent. Only a rough estimate, of course. I don't want to burden you with details. Long story short, your shares are worth three million now."

"Schillings?"

"Euros."

"That's got to be a mistake," Escher said. "I only invested ten thousand marks."

"No mistake," the ghost with the calculator replied, almost gruffly. "I've got it all here in front of me. Six thousand three hundred dollars. And forty-seven cents. That was the equivalent of your ten thousand marks at the time. It's here in black and white. It all tallies. Time has worked in your favor."

"Time?"

"Yes, time has worked. As has money. Time and money, you understand? I'll be honest with you, this isn't something you see every day. Actually, I've never seen something on this scale. With a single investment. We've checked it through three times. You bought at the best possible moment. Ten thousand marks. Back then. Five thousand euros. At the close of the stock market yesterday, you were valued at three million, twenty-seven thousand, four hundred and forty-two euros, and thirty-four cents. The US stock market won't be opening for another hour. Because of the time difference. Then we'll know exactly what the shares are worth today."

"The time difference," Escher said, surprised by his pointless repetition.

"It seems as if you still don't believe it," the man said, smiling almost compassionately.

"Three million?"

"Congratulations!"

"Thanks." Escher swallowed. "The idea that you can earn so much with books. I'm probably the most successful writer of all time!"

"What was your book called, if I may be so bold?"

"*A Sad Affair.*"

"How mistaken you can be," the advisor laughed.

Escher didn't know what to say.

"I expect you'll need some time to recover from the shock," Herr Nagy said. "But when you have, you should think about how you'd like to invest your fortune. The shares can go down in value too, you know. The market is particularly volatile at the moment. Regardless, it would be wise to diversify. Of course we'd be happy to advise you. I'll give you my card. Obviously, you now qualify for wealth management."

"What does that mean?"

"It means you don't have to go downstairs. You can make an appointment with me directly. By phone or via the website." He pushed his business card across the table but then took it back again and circled the telephone number with his blue ballpoint. "This is my cell. If you can't get through to me immediately, you can be sure I'll call you back. And of course I'll bring in the relevant specialists for your future investments. If you don't look after it properly, the money could dissipate pretty quickly."

"I'd like to withdraw it all," Escher said.

"Withdraw?"

"Yes, cash."

"Cash . . ."

In that moment such a racket came from the street that the windows in Tokyo rattled. Escher wondered whether the anger on the advisor's face was a symptom of the construction outside Tokyo now or because his valued client wanted to withdraw all his money.

"Would you allow me to offer a bit of old banking wisdom? Never make a big decision on the spur of the moment. We'd always recommend a forty-eight-hour cool-off period at least."

"I can understand that," Escher said. "But in my case, things are different. I had already decided before walking in that I'd take everything in cash."

After a long tussle, during which Herr Nagy emphatically advised him against such rashness, he explained to Escher that in any case he'd need a second appointment.

"Obviously we don't have that much cash on hand. For reasons of security, as I already said. We'll have to order the money. It'll be here tomorrow."

Emboldened by his status as a wealth management client, however, Escher said, "Maybe you could sort it out today? I mean, in any pharmacy you can order a prescription in the morning and have it filled by evening. So surely it must be possible to transport a few bundles of money from one branch to another. Otherwise, I could go to the branch where the cash is."

The bank advisor nodded slightly awkwardly and promised Escher to do his best. "If we're lucky I could organize the money today."

Escher almost laughed because Herr Nagy now sounded like a bank robber having to organize the dough.

"I'll need the help of my colleague, though," he said, sounding despondent once more.

Escher felt the hubris of a successful investor well up inside him, unsurprised that the doubter opposite him had sold his shares too early.

"My colleague is currently at the dentist's. He's been managing the pain with pills for weeks. But, of course, you can't keep doing that forever. May I suggest I call you in an hour? Then I'll be able to tell you for sure if we can do it today or not. I'm afraid the timing is very tight."

"I'd rather come by again in an hour," Escher said, thinking, *He'll make me wait for the phone call and then he'll palm me off and say it's too late.* He was surprised he was in such a hurry. Basically he didn't give a damn whether he got the money today or tomorrow morning. In any case he needed time to talk to the widow, organize the journey, and arrange the handover with the kidnappers.

In a café he ordered egg dumplings with a salad, devouring his lunch with the casual greed of a predator. His right hand shoveled the food into his mouth while his eyes ingested the book that lay beside his plate.

Then Corrado did appear again. Ala thought she'd heard him even before he entered the building. The distant tremor of the elevator starting up was followed by a groaning as the cab approached. Finally the elevator rattled to announce that it had once again avoided a fall. The banging of the doors and the scraping of Corrado's footsteps were replaced by the unfailing jangle of the prison warden's key that he used to unlock the door, after he'd tried in vain to kick it open.

"*A tavola, cucciolo mio,*" he greeted her every time in that same asshole tone, and even though Ala couldn't understand what he was saying, she wanted to kill him just for the *mio.*

But she maintained her composure. She kept staring at her book as if Corrado weren't there.

"Eat!"

"I'm afraid we're going to have to leave that for tomorrow," Ala read out loud and couldn't help laughing. What a shame that Corrado, the fool, couldn't understand those words. Otherwise, he would have realized how funny it was.

This is what the contrite Herr Nagy said to Escher when he returned to the bank an hour later. "My colleague had to wait two hours at the dentist's and now it's definitely too late."

Escher was startled by the anger that began to ferment inside him when he heard this. Had all that money corrupted him in a single hour? He felt like slamming his fist on the table but didn't know how to give vent to his anger. His new role as a wealth management client was still too unfamiliar. And so the bank advisor got there first and turned it around. "But, to be honest, it might be better for you this way."

"Are you saying it's better for me to wait?"

"You want the money in one-hundred-euro notes," Herr Nagy said, reminding Escher of the denomination he'd requested. "Do you have any idea how much thirty thousand one-hundred-euro notes weigh?"

"I expect you're about to tell me," Escher said, gradually losing patience with this fussy man. He just didn't want to hand over the cash.

One note weighs 0.035 ounces, the bank advisor informed the fledgling millionaire. Thirty thousand of them, therefore, would add up to just over sixty-seven pounds. He let his long but extremely nimble fingers clatter over the calculator, which to Escher looked as antiquated as the cash register in a country grocer's.

"Sixty-seven and a half pounds!" Nagy exclaimed, giving precision to his rapid estimate. "I thought it would be better if you were prepared for this. Because of the logistics of transporting it, if I may put it that way."

"I'll come with a granny cart tomorrow morning, then," Escher said. "Sixty-seven pounds . . . I'd break my back otherwise."

"Yes, a cart is a good idea," Herr Nagy said as he was making some further calculations.

It felt to Escher as if the bank advisor, to avoid going mad after his investment advice had been rejected along with the interest, risk, and profit calculations, quickly needed to calculate something else to compensate: "One hundred hundred-euro notes make a bundle half an inch thick—you might know these, they're typical hundred-euro bundles."

"Well, I don't exactly *know* them," Escher said. "But I've got an idea of what they're like."

"Yes, it's a compact bundle," Herr Nagy said, indicating the thickness with his thumb and forefinger. "In the banking world it's a familiar sight, of course. More familiar than three million, at any rate."

He looked at Escher expectantly, as if this comment might conjure a smile.

"Three million euros is three hundred such bundles," he said when there was no response. "That makes twelve feet. If you pile them all on top of each other. Which is my height plus five and a half feet."

"I'm sure there's room in the cart for ten piles," Escher said, his pride as a puzzle master not allowing this calculation to be taken out of his hands entirely. "That would then be ten times fourteen inches."

"Yes, that might be a bit too conservative," the bank advisor said, thinking out loud. "I don't think that the surface area of a shopping cart is big enough for ten piles. One note is six by three inches, *cum grano salis.*"

"*Cum grano salis,*" smirked Escher, buttered up once more by the pale Herr Nagy's antiquated phrase. "Did you go to a humanities-oriented school?"

"Sadly not," the bank advisor said. "I mean, I was always better at arithmetic than ancient languages. It wasn't the right sort of school for me. But . . ."

Too long ago to get worked up about it, his dismissive gesture said, and he accompanied it with a forbearing smile that seemed to be aimed at the absurd world beyond the pocket calculator.

"If you have two rows of five piles, that gives you sixteen by twelve," he said, returning to the matter at hand. "Yes, that might work. That might fit the surface area of a granny cart."

"I'll buy a cart that's big enough," said Escher, who'd now had enough of all this math. "When will the money be here?"

"Definitely by nine o'clock. Would you like a calendar?"

"A calendar? For me to jot down the appointment tomorrow morning?"

"No, I'm confident you'll remember that. But we've got a

rather charming pocket calendar for our private clientele. It's much in demand. Even the richest clients call us if they don't receive one."

"No thanks, I always remember my appointments by heart."

"How enviable."

On the way home Escher bought himself a violet granny cart, measured it when he got back, and came to the conclusion that ten piles would actually be better, to prevent the money from falling all over the place when transporting it because the piles were too loose. Then he put together Bruegel's *The Peasant Wedding*, perhaps because the weight of all the dishes being brought in and the beautiful arrangement of the plates on the boards used to carry them reminded him of his own transport logistics. Although Nellie Wieselburger had long ago tried to make him believe that the extra foot beneath the improvised tray belonged to the wedding guest helping to serve the dishes, he still hoped she was wrong. Every time he did this puzzle he expected a late guest who would come walking into the picture on this foot.

After Escher had prepared everything for the following morning, he went to bed. As he feared, however, he was far too wired to fall asleep. He tossed and turned for a while, then turned the light back on and hoped that reading would make him drowsy. He envied the character in the novel because she was doing precisely what he would love to—sleeping so deeply that she wasn't even woken by the clatter of the elevator.

Ala was startled from her sleep only after Corrado came crashing in. To top it all he wasn't alone; two women followed him into the room. The elder one was dressed in black from her headscarf to her shoes. Ala worried this might be the widow Madrisa whose food she'd refused so often. Despite her grandmotherly apparel, the widow was no older than Ala's mother. The younger woman was Ala's age. She held a wrought-iron baking dish in both hands.

"Ala!" the widow cried, but it sounded more like a pained sigh stirring from deep within her chest than a name. Corrado shoved her angrily to the side when she tried, with tears in her eyes, to embrace Ala. The widow didn't say a word to the ruffian, but shot him a withering look. The younger woman, however, lifted the iron dish and screamed so furiously at Corrado that Ala wouldn't have been surprised if she'd emptied its steaming contents over his head. Unafraid of Corrado, she explained that it was she who had contacted Ala as "Carlotta" via FAMILYTREE, before Corrado stole her identity. She, too, was looking for relatives of her own father, who'd been shot dead when she was three.

Ala hadn't looked in the mirror since she'd shattered it into a thousand pieces. But seeing the young woman who was her cousin, or noidea cousin once removed, Ala thought she'd finally taken leave of her senses. Nicoletta was her spitting image. Corrado freed her from this eerie moment. He went over to Ala's reflection and removed the lid from the dish. A heavenly smell filled the room. Ala's prison.

"*Melanzane alla parmigiana!*" Corrado announced like an ecstatic TV chef. "*A tavola, cucciolo mio!*"

"*Non parlare così, stronzo!*" Nicoletta snarled at him, putting the dish on the table.

Her outrage merely earned a laugh from the ape.

The gestures of those two were so telling that Ala didn't feel left out.

"*Dai, parla con lei!*" he hissed at Nicoletta.

The widow spoke calmly to Ala. She didn't wave her hands about, she just stroked Ala's forearm lovingly while Nicoletta translated her mother's words. Ala should have something to eat, she would be free soon. The money was already on its way. Madrisa wanted to serve up the food she'd brought for Ala but couldn't find a plate in the apartment and confronted Corrado. After making a gesture of contempt, he fetched the single spoon from the sink and offered it to Ala. As she wouldn't take it, in his frustration he flung the spoon into the dish before leaning pointedly against the door to the apartment, where he started playing a game on his phone.

"You have to eat," Nicoletta said. "They've already got the money together. It won't be long until you're free."

"I don't want to be free," Ala said. "My father's dead. And it's my fault."

Madrisa's face turned to stone. Nicoletta translated her mother's words, the utter seriousness of which Ala would have understood even without the translation. "Who says your father is dead?"

"It's written down."

"Written down?" Nicoletta repeated in disbelief.

She translated it for her mother, who repeated furiously, "*C'è scritto?*"

The widow gave a firm shake of the head. "*No, non c'è scritto!*"

"*Sì*," Ala spoke her first word of Italian. "*Sì, c'è scritto.*"

Madrisa talked insistently to her daughter, who translated for Ala. "Nothing is written before—"

"*Vaffanculo!*" cursed Corrado, who'd just failed to get a high score. He stomped over to the three women and pointed angrily at the deliciousness that Ala should now finally eat.

As Nicoletta refused to translate the rest of what he was saying and Ala continued to refuse to eat anything, he pushed the two women toward the door.

"What did she mean by that?" Ala cried out.

"By what?" Nicoletta asked.

"That nothing is written before. She said, 'Nothing is written before!' What was she trying to say? Before what?"

Finally losing his patience, Corrado herded the two of them out of the apartment.

"Before what?" Ala shouted in desperation.

But they were gone. All Ala heard was Corrado turning the key in the lock.

In her book it was written that her father was dead. She counted the number of pages left. Then, she read about how that Escher guy entered the bank with an empty granny cart, only to leave soon afterward with the cart bulging. He hurried back to his car, a white SEAT Alhambra, like a bank robber.

As she was mulling over whether it might not have been better to make twelve piles rather than ten, and calculating what the result might have been given a banknote of 5.78×3 in size, she didn't notice her hand reaching for the spoon in Madrisa's irresistible-smelling eggplant concoction, which she put away as slowly as she read, sentence by sentence, spoonful by spoonful.

With every mouthful she took, she was better able to concentrate. Her brain exited energy-saving mode and began to produce thoughts. Theories, deliberations, guesses, speculations. She guessed that Madrisa had been trying to tell her that you don't know what is written before you've read the final sentence. Before you've gotten to the end of the book. Now she had no difficulty following the words. They no longer swam before her eyes, and she read faster, making sure not to miss a single word.

Escher sped on down the freeway at seventy miles per hour. Since crossing the border he'd paid particular care not to exceed the speed limit. With three million euros in cash in tow, the last thing he wanted was to be stopped by the police. Even if the money was totally legitimate. He'd heard that Italians of all people, contrary to the stereotype, punished speeding with particular severity.

The line at the toll made him nervous, and he downloaded the audiobook. It wasn't really worth buying the book again because he'd already read most of it, but he didn't want to wait until evening to find out what happened next. To his surprise it downloaded without a hitch. He had problems, however, paying the toll. Although he'd gotten into the right lane—not the one for trucks or for those with an annual pass—his card was denied. Herr Nagy had initially offered to upgrade his credit card, but with Escher withdrawing his entire fortune, he hadn't mentioned it again. And his old credit card was cursed. Escher wondered whether, now that he had a normal amount of savings in his account, he could still call the wealth management number with his problem.

To his relief he saw that the machine took cash. But he could scrape together only thirty-seven euros and the toll was forty-one! In the door he found a fifty-cent coin and that was it. He couldn't believe it. Even with three million euros in cash, he didn't have enough on him to pay the toll.

He was forced to go to the effort of getting out of the car and extracting a one-hundred-euro note from the cart in the back seat. To his astonishment, nobody honked at him and he was able to unhurriedly open the cart and pluck a banknote from a bundle held together by a band. There was almost something menacing about the silence of the line growing ever longer behind him. Escher found that despite his steady nerves, it was only with difficulty that he suppressed a screaming fit when he realized the machine wouldn't accept such a large denomination. Now the driver of the car right behind him finally did lay on the horn. Pressing the red button to talk to someone, Escher found himself overwhelmed by a flurry of Italian. He realized he had to back out and fight his way through to the change kiosk. The moment he put the car into reverse his phone rang.

Nellie Wieselburger's name appeared on the screen. As he'd switched off his voicemail some time ago, the ringing didn't stop, but it was drowned out by the symphony of beeping that erupted when he forced the entire line of cars to reverse.

Only an hour later, after he'd changed the money but discovered at another tollbooth that his card now worked perfectly, did he remember Nellie. He was still annoyed by the fact that she'd persistently let the phone ring for minutes on end.

"Thanks for calling back," she greeted him with extraordinary politeness.

He could sense at once that something wasn't right.

"No problem. I couldn't answer before because I was parking and then—"

"Look, there's something crucial I've got to talk to you about."

He felt like hanging up again. Crucial things were, to his mind, unpleasant. Especially when they were announced in this way. In such a Wieselburgerish way. He should have called her Nellie Crucialburger in his book. Maybe then it would have been a success.

"I'm afraid I'm not at home right now."

"That's okay. We can just chat on the phone for a bit. Or am I disturbing you?"

"No, no, it's fine."

The truck behind him flashed its headlights because he was driving ever more slowly. He put his foot down and overtook a few vehicles before slotting back into the other lane and switching to cruise control.

"We've known each other for a really long time now, and somehow I don't like the way we treat each other," she said, gearing herself up for a New Year's resolution in the middle of the year.

"Aha," Escher meant to say. But suddenly he was overcome by fatigue, and the first *A* instead lapsed into a throaty exhalation, reducing the intended melodiousness of his reply to a wheeze. Like the final breath of a suffocating man.

"And, sure, I'm not innocent either," Nellie said. "I used to pretend that it didn't bother me in the slightest that you made fun of me in your book. Do you remember how I always glossed over it and pretended it was just the name Mitzi that upset me?"

"Sure, but I didn't mean to offend you by calling your character Mitzi."

"That's exactly what I'm getting at," she said. "I only got so worked up about the name because I didn't want to let on about the rest of it. It was a red herring, do you see?"

"Aha."

"Did you really think those snide comments you made about my funeral orations didn't bother me at all?"

"It's so long ago. My memory is very hazy."

"Mine isn't, Escher. I remember it very well. Empathy chat 'cobbled together from the same building blocks of condolence.' Unsympathetic prose machine. Do you think stuff like that just passed me by, without leaving its mark?"

For the first time in his life, he considered what a beautiful voice she had. Not that callous, overbearing tone that everybody seemed to have these days. But more in the direction of beautiful. He was in a dilemma. On the one hand he wanted her speech to finish, but on the other he was very happy for her to continue speaking.

"Yes, well, it was a bit . . . it was all meant in jest, Nellie."

"It wasn't funny at all," Nellie said very soberly, without

cutting him short or raising her voice. "I actually think you've got a problem when someone gets close to you. I mean, we got on really well for a time. And then suddenly you stopped reaching out. Never had time."

"There was always something."

"There is always something, Escher. And you lied to me all the time too."

"No. Or at most when it was the simpler route. With the explanations and all that."

"Well, I had my pride and so I decided to spend time with other people. And then you came along with that book."

"Come on, there were several years in between. You don't need to connect the two."

"Anyway, I think we could start treating each other like human beings again. I'm not looking for any more than that."

"Yes, let's do that."

"Just be honest with each other."

"Sure."

"You don't need to sound so sheepish. I'm not saying this to get at you. What are you thinking right now?"

"You don't want to know."

"How do you know I don't want to know?"

Escher felt himself in the throes of a death wish. He was on the verge of telling Nellie Wieselburger the truth.

"Well, how should I put it . . . I'm thinking that it's not always possible to be honest, Nellie. Take someone in witness protection, for example. Now, they have to keep everything secret. Their past and so on. They can't be honest. In that case dishonesty can even be proof of love."

Nellie laughed. "Oh, Escher. You really are deranged! Can't you even think of a more far-fetched example?"

There was silence for a while.

"What are you doing right now? You said you're not at home."

"I just need to pop down to Italy. There are three million euros in the back of my car and I've got to free a hostage."

"Right, I see," Nellie said sadly. "It's impossible to get anywhere with you. But I'm glad I told you, at least."

"I'm glad too," Escher said.

He wondered whether this was a lie or the truth.

"Do you know what struck me? You've got a very lovely speaking voice."

"A lovely speaking voice!" she laughed. "That's such an insult. It's like telling someone, 'You're so photogenic.'"

While Escher pondered whether this was true, Nellie said a warm goodbye and hung up.

He realized, to his surprise, that sixty miles had passed in a flash. Numbed by his phone call, Escher also drove straight past Florence, where he'd intended to stay the night. Not long afterward he felt so tired that he took a room in the first hotel he came to off the motorway. At least nobody in this dump tried to help him with his luggage. He lifted the granny cart up next to him in the double bed, wrapped his arms around it, and immediately fell asleep. At four a.m. he woke up and got back on the road, skipping breakfast.

He had a double espresso and a croissant at a gas station, which he'd just managed to reach with the reserve tank. His credit card worked perfectly. He bought a can of chilled espresso for the journey and only then did he remember the audiobook. He fast-forwarded to the page at which his book was lying face down at home.

Ala woke up because Corrado had come back into her room. At first, she thought she'd just nodded off at the table. But it was light outside. To her astonishment she saw that the dish was empty.

Corrado laughed idiotically when he saw how much she'd eaten.

"*Stronzo!*" she barked, using the same word Nicoletta had hurled at him the previous day.

Even to herself, Ala's tone sounded unfamiliar. Strength had returned to her body. Her voice sounded powerful; it was as if she'd transformed overnight into Nicoletta, her doppelgänger.

As if he'd mistaken her for Nicoletta too, Corrado said something in Italian. And only when Ala stared at him blankly did he instruct her in English to pack.

"What?"

"You're free."

"How stupid do you think I am, *stronzo*?" she bellowed. "You're intending to kill me!"

"No, we're not. Pack everything up! We don't have much time."

As she didn't move a muscle, Corrado himself gathered up

the few things they'd let her keep and stuffed them into Ala's backpack.

Then he thrust the backpack at her chest and she instinctively threw both arms around it. At the same moment he grabbed her upper arm and, ignoring Ala's angry cries of pain, dragged her out of the apartment and shoved her toward the elevator. Not even when they were both inside did he let go.

"You're! Hurting! Me!" Ala screamed in German.

With a laugh he offered up a poor imitation of what she'd said.

By comparison with Corrado, the rattling of the elevator sounded almost intelligent. After the rough landing on the first floor, the elevator was a couple of feet too low down and the door wouldn't open; Corrado cursed. They went all the way back up, then down again.

Finally, they got into the car that was waiting for them. Its engine was running, and it pulsated with loud music. It was the same vehicle that had brought her here. The driver was the same too. He sported a new haircut but sadly hadn't changed his aftershave.

Corrado showed him a bloody scratch that Ala had given him and said something; Ala recognized only the words *puttana* and *stupida*. The driver gave a dirty laugh and drove off.

Ala got annoyed when they spoke Italian. In English she said, "I feel sick!"

"You've eaten too much," Corrado chuckled.

"I'm going to throw up!"

From the sudden emergency brake and the care with which they helped Ala out of the car, she sensed the great love both men held for their car.

"You stink," Corrado said when they were back in the car. "That's the worst thing on earth! Having to watch another person vomit!"

"Why don't you say something nice for a change?" Ala heard herself say. "I'm fourteen years old, surely you can say something nice to me."

"*You* say something nice to *me*! I'm twenty-three—*you* say something nice!"

"I asked first."

Corrado laughed. "You always have to have the last word, don't you? Okay, when the money arrives you'll be free."

"And when is the money arriving?"

"Your turn!"

"What?"

"You have to say something nice."

"I need to go to the bathroom."

"What?" the driver cried in horror.

"We're almost there," Corrado said.

"How much longer?" Ala asked.

"An hour," Corrado guessed as the driver said, "Two hours."

"I can't wait that long. It would be a shame to pee on your car seat."

"Oh, God! First you have to be sick, then you have to piss! What kind of a baby are you?"

"You can take your pick," Ala said.

"I can't let you out without putting handcuffs on you," Corrado threatened.

"Just damn well stop!" Ala howled.

The driver suggested they stop at the next bridge. "She can't run away there."

Corrado didn't say yes and didn't say no, which was as good as saying yes. When they were on the bridge, he opened the passenger and rear doors.

"That's how we do it, you see? You're screened from the front and the back."

"What about you two?"

Both men laughed idiotically.

"We're like doctors," Corrado said. "Our eyes don't count."

"Get out the other side and keep looking at the road. I can't run away from here anyway."

As they were afraid of Cousin Nicoletta, whom Ala was channeling, they got out of the driver's side and watched the juggernauts thundering past a couple of feet away.

No sooner was Ala back in the car than the two of them decided that they might as well make use of the opportunity too. They got out again and, standing side by side, took a leak onto the cars racing along the road under the bridge. Ala once heard that a boy had died when his cheerfully dispatched urine hit the power line of a railway. She prayed that the same might happen to these two, but she wasn't much of a believer and nothing happened.

The rest of the journey passed without interruption. Just as Ala was thinking that they would be driving forever through this alien landscape, from one ruined village to the next, they stopped outside a dilapidated stone house. It looked as if it hadn't been inhabited since a couple of earthquakes ago. All the windows and doors were bricked up. A stone statue of the Madonna that stood in a recess beside the door was so weather-beaten, it might have been standing sentry there since before the birth of Christ.

Ala's bodyguards greeted the Holy Virgin with a sanctimonious look, at which the Madonna moved slowly and silently to one side, leaving a gap in the wall between herself and the blocked-up door.

"*Miracolo!*" Corrado laughed. "Do you know who came up with that? The remote control and everything? The retinal scan and everything? Long before the others had it? Who do you think designed all this? A genius! A technological genius!"

He took her arm, but only as firmly as any normal person would. Anyone seeing them might have thought this was a bridegroom taking his bride to his parents' house for the first time.

"Your father!" Corrado said in awe. "Only he knows how it works."

The Madonna closed the house behind them again, and at the very moment the daylight was blocked out, an elevator door opened before them.

"*Miracolo!*" Corrado rejoiced once more.

The elevator smoothly took them several floors down where

they entered a luxurious residential space. Like a hotel lobby, the guests were greeted with relaxing music, and the sophisticated lighting made them blind to the lack of windows. Because Ala had never stepped on such a precious carpet before, she wanted to take off her shoes, but Corrado gave a dismissive wave of the hand and opened a door. This led to an elegant apartment that was illuminated by a huge aquarium. Instead of windows, a screen hung on each wall, showing the landscape they'd just driven through.

"You're staying here," Corrado said. "We'll see each other again tomorrow."

"You said I was free."

"Tomorrow. When the money arrives."

He locked the door behind her.

Ala gazed at the fish and waited. The creatures gawping through the glass reminded her of her own time behind the tower-block window. Waiting for someone to come in, or for a telephone to ring, or for a voice to be heard. But nothing of the sort happened, and the sight of the fish put her so at ease that she was emboldened to snoop around the apartment. On the glass coffee table was a bowl with green and purple grapes, mini bananas, and fruits she'd never set eyes on before. The fridge was full of delicacies, and the espresso machine blinked invitingly. She opened a cupboard where she found a dressing gown and flip-flops. The bathroom was so elegant that she hardly dared enter it. In truth she turned on the bathtub tap only to see if water was really flowing there. When the bath was full she soaked in it and waited until the water went cold. The mirror reminded her of Nicoletta and the soft eyes of the widow Madrisa.

The bed where she was to sleep was big enough for an entire family. She wondered how they'd gotten the monstrosity in here in the first place. She counted the pillows so she'd be able to tell Selina Katharina how many there were. Then she got up and tried counting the fish in the aquarium. Then she lay back down on the bed and counted the number of pages left in the book. But counting didn't help; it was impossible to sleep in a bed like this. And because Madrisa had claimed that nothing is written before . . . she set about the final pages.

Although Escher had paid heed to the speed limit throughout his journey, he was stopped by the police two hours from Naples. He must have been too distracted by the audiobook because when he saw the blue light flickering in the rearview mirror, his speedometer needle was, to his amazement, pointing at more than a hundred miles per hour.

Panicked, he had the ludicrous urge to flee. How could he explain the three million euros to the police? Sure, over time he'd be able to prove that the money was his rather than booty from a gang robbery. But until then he'd probably stew in a cell and it would be too late for Ala.

He braked and let the police car overtake him. In its rearview mirror he saw two red illuminated signs frantically flashing in turn.

FOLLOW US!

SEGUICI!

FOLLOW US!

SEGUICI!

Escher followed them. He rolled the window down so they wouldn't smell the sweat of his fear. Maybe there was still a chance that they'd check only his papers. Or they'd just glance in the trunk and find the small suitcase with his clothes, ignoring the harmless granny cart in the back seat. If he stayed calm, the possibility remained that he could escape with no more than a fright. Fortunately, he'd taken out three hundred euros at the motorway toll. If he showed remorse and paid the fine in cash without any fuss, maybe they wouldn't be interested in the cart at all.

SEGUICI!

FOLLOW US!

SEGUICI!

FOLLOW US!

The police car turned into a parking lot and Escher followed them.

"STOP HERE," the sign ordered. Escher put his foot on the brake. Before the police car had fully come to a stop, the officer on the passenger side leaped out of the vehicle. Escher was sweating bullets. In his rearview mirror he saw that Nellie Wieselburger was right. From this angle he did indeed bear a striking resemblance to the beheaded Saint John by Giovan Francesco Maineri. All that was missing was the silver bowl.

The officer greeted Escher with exaggerated propriety and demanded to see his documents. He gave them a thorough inspection, comparing the photograph with the driver before him, and asked if he was Franz Escher.

"*Si*," Escher said, "I am Franz Escher."

Only then did he realize that in his panic he'd forgotten to turn off his audiobook. He was going to cautiously reach down—so the policeman didn't get the wrong idea that he was going for a gun—and switch it off, when the police officer handed back his documents. He asked Escher to get out and open the trunk. No mention had yet been made of the speeding. He let Escher open the small case and saw that it contained only two shirts, underwear, and a toiletry bag. Then he asked Escher to open the rear doors. On the back seat lay the violet cart. The officer was giving it a hard stare, as if he thought there might be a bomb inside, when the audiobook narrator said that Ala was startled by a knock at her door.

Ala didn't dare respond to the knock. She couldn't unlock the door anyway. She listened spellbound, wondering whether anyone would say anything. Then she heard the door being opened.

Having listened to Corrado talk about the boss, Ala had pictured him quite differently. The old man with white hair who came in the room was almost as small and slender as a child. Nor would the mass of his unruly hair have been out of place on the head of a teenager. Its snow-white hue made it look almost like a wig on the translucent parchment skin of his face.

"I'm Gino," he said, offering a friendly hand to Ala.

His suit fitted him perfectly, the felt slippers in which his feet shuffled across the floor being the only jarring note.

"You look just like your grandmother, Ala. Just like her. How are you?"

Although it was unsurprising that he knew her name, she still felt goose bumps.

"I'm pleased that you can keep me company for a while."

Because Ala didn't know what to say, she asked how he spoke such perfect English.

"I spent many years with my uncle's family in Chicago."

Ala nodded. She could imagine the uncle.

"But I've been back for more than twenty years now."

"You came back from America only twenty years ago? You must have been there a long time."

Ala didn't mean to offend him, but even twenty years ago he must have been too old to start a new life. She was appalled when it struck her that he might be insulted by her comment.

"No, no, I've been back much longer than that," the old man explained kindly. "I've been in this basement for twenty years. But there's nothing I want for. The police won't find my hiding place. You can only open up from the inside. Or with your eyes—if you greet the Madonna piously enough that she's able to peer into your soul," he said with a soft smile. "On my screens here I can see everything that's going on outside."

"And no one can see the cameras?"

The old man shook his head with a contented grin. Wistfully, he said, "Elio built it all. The camera in the Madonna and everything else. The circuits. The retinal scan, do you understand? Even though he was still such a young man! He was far ahead of his time."

"Elio?"

"Yes, your father. He was always—I can't put it any other

way—far ahead of his time! Even as a young man he was skilled at everything to do with remote control systems, cameras, and all that new stuff. Anything that had the slightest connection to electricity. Whether it was electricity or electronics, Elio was ahead of all the rest. I owe my freedom to him. He flew the medicines into prison that allowed me to leave in a hearse. It pained me greatly that he betrayed us. That broke all our hearts."

Ala swallowed.

"I ought to have had my suspicions when the medicines arrived only on the second attempt. He didn't make mistakes, you see. But at least he was smart enough not to reveal where I live," the old man smiled. "Elio was so smart. He knew that this was his life insurance policy. He told them everything, but not about my hideaway. Would you play a game with me?"

"What sort of game?"

"I play lots of games here. I mean, it's a bit boring. Even though I have regular visitors. I've got so many grandchildren. They all come to visit me. They have to play with me too. Even my tailor has to play with me when he visits."

He smiled meekly to suggest that the children and the tailor weren't exactly thrilled to be playing games with him, but he enjoyed their company nonetheless.

"What do you play with them?" Ala asked.

"The children like playing video games best. But I'm still old-fashioned. Do you do puzzles?"

"Puzzles? Sure!"

"That's good. You'll be given breakfast now, and then Federica will bring you over to me and we can do a puzzle together."

He went out to call his housekeeper, who served Ala two croissants with blood-orange marmalade on a silver tray. When asked whether she'd like tea or coffee, Ala just replied, "*Si*," and, to her delight, was given both. Federica said, "*Buon appetito!*" and no sooner had she closed the door behind her than Ala scarfed down the delicious breakfast and searched in her book for the last lines she could remember reading.

Escher felt his legs trembling. Worried he might fall over, he supported himself on the door of the Alhambra, just in case. With his other hand he wanted to hold on to the police officer who was sternly looking inside the car and pointing at the granny cart.

"Is that the money?" he asked, without looking at Escher.

"I'm sorry?"

"Is that the money?"

"What do you mean?"

"You shouldn't be driving so quickly with that money in the car," the officer said. "If you were pulled over by the wrong officer, it'd be gone."

He peered briefly inside the cart to make sure they'd stopped the right person. Then he returned to the police car without another word and got back in. The illuminated sign in the rear windscreen booted up again, proclaiming its seductive message:

FOLLOW US!

SEGUICI!

FOLLOW US!

SEGUICI!

Shaking, Escher followed the police car and heard from his car's speakers that Gino's housekeeper Federica was knocking at Ala's bedroom door. She was visibly delighted that her guest had eaten everything up, even the jar of blood-orange marmalade. Taking the tray from the table, she escorted the guest over to Gino's living room.

Ala had never seen such a fairytale room in her life. It looked like an underground castle full of treasures. A chamber full of exquisite furniture and rugs, with vases and candelabras in an enchanted palace. On the walls hung oil paintings in magnificent gold frames, which reminded Ala of her school trip to the famous noidea museum. But here the paintings didn't have to be protected from sunlight because, as in her guest apartment, huge screens replaced the windows, offering a 360-degree view of the surrounding countryside. On one of them Ala could see Corrado's parked car. Corrado himself and the driver were standing beside it, seemingly waiting for something.

Gino stood at the head of a table big enough for ten state visitors. But there were just the two of them. Gino and Ala. Gino had already spread the puzzle out on the table and put together a few fragments of what appeared to be a gigantic picture. She noticed that he was wearing white gloves. And that these puzzle pieces were cut differently from normal. They weren't the typical bizarre shapes she was familiar with, but small squares that, with their size, looked more like a game of memory than a puzzle.

Gino handed her a pair of fine white gloves.

"We have to do the puzzle with gloves," he explained. "It's too valuable. You shouldn't touch it with your fingers."

Ala didn't ask why the pieces were so delicate. But she realized that the small squares were not cardboard pieces manufactured by a machine. Some were a bit frayed at the edges or not cut to precision. When she picked up a light-blue square with a blue corner, she noticed it was softer than expected. More like some stiff material. The surface wasn't as smooth as a printed puzzle, either, but looked as if it had been actually painted.

"I'm probably being overcautious," Gino said. "I expect it will never be able to return to its original condition. From a technical point of view that's not possible. But you never know. Maybe one day it will be possible to make a complete picture out of it again. New technologies. Computers! Lasers! Electronic magic! That's why I touch it only with gloves. We never know what the future will bring."

"It isn't written down," Ala said.

"No, not written down," the frail old man agreed, adding another piece to one of the fragments that were emerging at various points on the table. "It's in the stars, Ala."

Gino kept working on the puzzle. Ala was amazed by the tranquil certainty with which he set down the squares. She looked at him for a while, wondering how many times over the past twenty years he'd put together the innumerable pieces into a whole picture.

"Help me," Gino said. "It's fun, you'll see."

"How many times have you done this puzzle?" Ala now ventured to ask.

Gino smiled. "I've lost count, Ala. It's a nice diversion. Down here, time takes on a different meaning."

"Like a loop?"

"How did you know?"

"I read it in a book."

She picked up one of the square pieces and tried to find where it fit.

"That's an edge bit," Gino said, smiling. "You can tell because the edges are roughly cut."

He took it from her hand and ran his gloved fingers over the uneven surface. Then he set it on the edge of the table. "This table was made to order. That's also why it's got these raised edges, so nothing falls off. Do you see?"

Ala was taken aback. The table was almost ten feet long and twice as wide as a normal dining table. She'd never seen such a large puzzle before.

"It's 78 by 106 inches," the old man said, smiling. "It tells the story of the birth of Christ. Are you Catholic?" he asked, without looking up from the puzzle.

"I think we're noidea sort of ecumenical?" Ala said.

"It's a devotional painting. I'm afraid I don't have a copy of the complete picture here to help you. I've got it in my head. I must have put it together a thousand times."

Ala looked for another square, picked one up, put it down again, and took another. The old man pointed to the middle of the stylish wooden table, which was still completely empty. "Here's the face of the Madonna," he said, indicating the shining surface of the table. "She's sitting on the stable floor, having given birth to Our Savior. Her right hand is on her belly." He briefly let his own right hand circle around the place where the Madonna's right hand ought to be. "And lying on the ground is the newborn child. Not on the straw itself, but on a white cloth."

"Is the woman naked?" Ala asked.

The old man laughed. "Of course not! She's no woman, she's the Holy Virgin! She's wearing a red dress and a white blouse, like women used to wear here, you know? To her right is St. Joseph. He's sitting. But you only see him from behind. He's blond! Or as white-haired as me. Depending on how you wish to see it. But his legs are so muscular that he's most likely a young blond man," the boss Gino said, smiling again and putting another square in place. "Caravaggio must have derived great pleasure from these legs."

"What's Caravaggio?"

"The painter, my child," the old man said. "That was his name. Michelangelo Merisi, known as Caravaggio. After the place he came from. Have you never heard of him?"

"Yes, I think I have. At school or something."

She remembered that she'd read the name in her book. But before she could mention this to Gino, he was already talking again.

"A great artist. The conqueror of Mannerism! Sadly, two thugs stole the picture from the oratory in Palermo. Stupid scumbags!

Just imagine, the ruffians cut out the canvas! And not only that. When they realized you can't sell such a famous painting they cut it into four pieces! Can you believe it?"

Ala shook her head sadly, even though she didn't care.

"They thought it would be easier to sell the pieces." The boss of bosses stared forlornly at the empty table where, in his mind's eye, he could see the finished picture. "There are too many idiots working in our line of business. We were able to save the picture from those blunderheads. But there wasn't anything we could do. We couldn't make it whole again. You can't make something that's been cut up whole again. Nobody can. What's cut up can be saved only by cutting it up even more, do you understand?"

Ala nodded even though she didn't.

"You have to keep cutting it, Ala, into so many pieces until it becomes whole again. That's what we did. An inch by an inch. Do you know how many squares that makes in a painting that's 78 by 106 inches?"

"A thousand?" Ala hazarded a guess.

"Eight thousand one hundred and ninety squares!" Gino said proudly. "I put it together every day, my sweetheart. By now it's become so familiar that the uncut picture would seem wrong to me. Only in here," he said, smiling and tapping the side of his head, "does it become whole again!"

Ala mulled over what the old man had just said. She was going to ask him something, but before the thought had crystallized he was back with his puzzle.

"You see St. Joseph only from behind because he's talking to

the bearded man. He's standing here, to the right of St. Francis,"
Gino said, pointing to the half of the table that was still completely empty. "And standing on the other side, to the left of the
Madonna, is St. Lawrence. He's holding onto the gridiron he
was burned on. And behind him a cow is peering inquisitively at
the baby Jesus."

The boss, who was sentenced in absentia for seventy-three
murders, laughed about the cow. "A stupid cow! Next to the
Madonna!" He shook his head in disbelief. "And flying up
there is an angel. A wonderful angel. Just like your father when
he flew me the wonderful medicines. Albeit on the second attempt. He kept the first shipment, that cheeky devil."

Like a karate fighter measuring up against his opponent, Gino
held his outstretched hand over the center of the table.

"The angel's wing is here, right in the middle of the picture.
It's vertical. A vertical wing. You can almost hear the swishing of
the air," the old man laughed. "And the angel's arm is pointing
down at the newborn Redeemer. The other hand is pointing up
at God. And here . . . !"

On the screen showing the driveway, where nothing had
moved until now, Ala noticed a car gradually getting bigger. A
police car. Behind it came another car. A white SEAT Alhambra.
Ala knew this model because Selina Katharina's father also drove
one, although his was black. Both vehicles disappeared, only to
appear immediately on the other screen, which until now had
shown nothing but Corrado's parked car. The SEAT Alhambra
stopped in front of Corrado's vehicle, blocking it out completely.

The police car turned around and headed back down the drive. In the rear windscreen of the shrinking police car an illuminated sign flashed: "*Ciao Gino!*"

Gino didn't allow himself to be distracted. He pointed at the upper-left corner of the table. "This is where the white banner runs, fluttering from the angel's hand. You know those advertising banners flown from small aircraft?"

Ala shook her head.

"I don't think they have so many of them these days," Gino said. "They used to be common. Advertising for an event or a new Fiat. Small aircraft would fly over villages, trailing banners behind them. The new Fiat Punto. Or a Pavarotti concert. A Primo Carnera fight. Or the Giro d'Italia. Or a race at Mugello."

Deep in his memories, the old man seemed to have forgotten the puzzle, but then he said, "One of those banners is flying from the angel's hand too. Here! It says, GLORIA IN ECCELSIS DEO. With two *C*'s, not an *X*. That's how it used to be written. So, if you've got a letter, this is where it goes."

Just as Ala was about to pick up a letter fragment, there came a knock at the door. Without turning his head, the old man said softly, as if he were talking to Ala or the angel, "Come in. But open the door slowly; otherwise, the draught will blow all the pieces around."

Corrado entered with a granny cart, lifted it with a groan, and tipped the heavy contents onto the empty middle of the table. The bundles of money landed roughly where the Madonna's face was going to go. "We've already counted it. It's three million."

"Take it away!" the boss snapped angrily. "It doesn't belong here."

Corrado obeyed like a dog, and in no time at all the money had disappeared from the table again, to be stored in a safe.

The old man gave Ala a loving smile, pulled off his gloves, and offered her his hand. "I suppose that means it's time for us to say goodbye, my dear child. You're being picked up."

He gave Corrado a few more instructions about what to do with the cart, then said to Ala, "I'm going to give you a little gift so that you don't take just bad memories away from here."

Ala shook his hand, left Gino's fairytale castle, and went over to the guest apartment, where Federica had brought fresh fruit to replace yesterday's. Ala chewed a few grapes and waited. Corrado had stayed with Gino but rapped at her door shortly afterward. Only now did it occur to Ala that he'd knocked respectfully at Gino's earlier. He gestured with his head that she was to follow him. Corrado left the door to the guest apartment open and went ahead to the elevator. Ala was surprised that he hadn't grabbed her by the arm to drag her along. She couldn't believe she was going to be freed and she was moving almost as slowly as Corrado. Then the magic elevator took her so quietly and gently back up that Ala was still waiting for it to move when the door opened on the first floor.

Outside, the SEAT Alhambra was waiting with its engine running. Normally Ala hated it when a driver let the engine of a parked car idle. Once she'd even said something to a complete stranger. She and Selina Katharina had shrieked at the idiot behind the wheel, "Engine off!" But she wasn't bothered by that sort of thing right now. She didn't care, even though she couldn't know that the man behind the wheel was blameless in this respect. He'd been given the order to wait for her with the engine running. Not only was the engine on, an audiobook was playing, which Ala could hear when Corrado yanked open the trunk of the Alhambra.

At the very moment when Corrado opened the trunk and chucked the granny cart into the car, the voice of the audiobook narrator said that Corrado threw the violet cart into the back of the Alhambra with such force that it clattered loudly and shut the trunk. The narrator and Ala's brain then paused.

Corrado wrenched open the passenger door and placed his hand on his hostage's head, like a policeman protecting a detainee—but with a roughness that suggested the opposite.

"*Gute Reise!*" Corrado wished her. His voice was perfectly audible even though all the doors and windows were now closed. It was coming from the car speakers.

The narrator did Corrado's voice very well.

And a moment later, the completely different voice of Gino.

"Bring me the book Ala left in the guest apartment," Gino ordered when Corrado went back to see him in the basement.

"It's in a foreign language, I'm afraid," Corrado said apologetically when he returned.

"Can't you find it in Italian? Or in English?"

Two minutes later Corrado had downloaded the book in English. Before Escher and Ala, who had fallen asleep in the SEAT Alhambra while listening, had left the Aspromonte, Gino began to read.

Thirteen hours later, Gino had gotten to the last page. As day was about to break, Escher, who had driven through the entire night save for a gas stop, headed to the large cemetery on the edge of his home city. Ala woke up as he was parking outside the closed cemetery gate. Either she wasn't yet fully awake or she'd heard the occasional passage while asleep, but with a sleepwalker's lack of inhibition she followed Escher to the cemetery gate, which, as every funeral orator knew, was never locked. They continued to her father's grave, where the headstone had in the meantime been installed without ceremony or funeral oration.

Standing by the grave was a man. He was gazing at the cross, absorbed in his thoughts, and turned his head only when Escher and Ala approached. Despite the gloom Escher could see at once that it was the electrician. Ala ran to her father and hugged him. Escher stood awkwardly beside the two of them and read the inscription on the grave cross:

MARKO STEINER 1982–2024

Not only were the graves here different from those in the cemetery at Aspromonte, where the star witness had said goodbye to his former life. It was also light out. At the grave of Elio Russo (1981–2002) it had still been night time. An hour before sunrise. Without Falcone's flashlight they'd never have been able to find the grave. And whereas then he'd stood beside his own grave with the investigating judge, now he was standing beside his grave with his daughter and her liberator, Escher.

The three of them looked at the inscription announcing his death.

"How did you do that?" his daughter asked.

Marko Steiner smiled without taking his eyes off the date of his death. He'd resolved never to lie to his daughter again. But she could be put off with a smile until a tolerable version of the truth was on offer. And, for Ala, this special smile that took possession of her father's lips was enough to predict the words that would come from the smile. It went without saying that she took the words out of his mouth:

"Three-Card Monte?"

Her father nodded.

"Correct," he said. "Three-Card Monte. Also known as?—"

"Lucky Seven."

Escher smiled to himself, for as a funeral pro and orator, it went without saying that you didn't interrupt the moments of comprehension.

They stood beside the grave a while longer, as if someone who'd been buried more than once deserved their full attention and due reverence, when bidding farewell.

Only when daylight had finally won its battle with the night did Ala ask where her mother was.

"She's waiting in the car," Marko Steiner said. "Everything's packed."

"Packed?"

"Yes, we've got to move. You can choose a new name."

"Where's the car?"

Escher wondered where they were moving to. As if reading

his mind, the electrician turned to him and said, "We're moving to the most beautiful city."

"The most beautiful city? I'd like to move there too."

"Then maybe we'll meet again," the electrician said, smiling, as Ala's eyes were already scanning the area for the parking lot. Escher realized it was time. He wanted to say goodbye to the two of them. He would have found it awkward to accept the thanks of the widow, who wasn't a widow anymore. He also rebuffed the electrician's thanks. And he withdrew from the handshake when he remembered the gift he'd left in the car.

"I've just got to give you Gino's gift."

"We don't accept gifts from that sort," the electrician said. "It belongs to you."

"No, it's for Ala."

"And she's giving it to the man who set her free. Isn't that right?" he asked his daughter.

Ala nodded.

"Please don't worry. I mean, you've given us three million," he reassured Escher. "Anyway, we don't have to say bye right now. I'll pop by quickly on our way out of the city. Your outlet still needs fixing."

"That's not necessary," Escher said.

"Oh, it is. Never leave a job half done. That's how I was brought up. Besides, you can't be having to unplug the kettle each time you want to use the coffee machine. And there's the loose connection! I can't understand how you've been able to live with something like that for so long."

Like when she was little, his daughter took his hand, something she hadn't done for at least three years.

"You go on," the electrician said to Escher. "We're going to pray for a bit and we'll meet you there."

"Do you really want to make the detour?"

"You can't move without a detour. It brings bad luck."

"Aren't you worried that I'll flip the circuit breakers again?"

"Wouldn't be a problem," Elio said with a smile.

Escher drove home, and although he was so exhausted that he could barely stand, he took the granny cart out of the car straightaway. It was heavy, but not as heavy as before, and, taking a peek on the sidewalk, he was surprised that 8,190 canvas squares didn't weigh more.

As he waited for the elevator, Escher put Gino's present to one side and opened his mailbox. He imagined it must be stuffed full after his epic journey. But in truth he hadn't been away for long and all he found was a small, plain padded envelope. Inside was a tiny object in bubble wrap. He almost failed to notice the accompanying letter that had been squashed into the envelope.

"We apologize for any inconvenience that you may have experienced as a result of our production error," the manufacturer of *The Creation of Adam* puzzle wrote, to whom Escher had written several letters of complaint over the years. The company had gotten to the bottom of the missing piece that had left a hole between the forefingers of God and Adam. "During a major servicing of our machinery we discovered that due to a technical defect this piece was eaten by our punching machine. Over the course of several years, a mountain of pieces had collected inside the machine. We should like to thank you for your feedback and we wish you the greatest of pleasure with your now complete *The Creation of Adam.*"

Not knowing what to do with the piece that had been missing for so long, when the elevator arrived he stuffed it into the envelope and put this back into his mailbox, which he locked. It was too late now anyway.

He wanted to ring Nellie Wieselburger right away. But when he finally got into his apartment he realized that it was still very early. Instead of calling her, he pulled the cart into the middle of the living room and took a photo of it. "Your phone call made me think. I don't know if I'll manage to become a better person. But at any rate I've brought you a present back from Italy. It's in the granny cart (see photo). Please let me know when you've got time for the handover."

He felt like lying down for a few hours' sleep. But the electrician would be there soon and he didn't want to miss him. To be on the safe side, Escher checked once more that the doorbell wasn't turned off. Then he tipped the eight thousand pieces out on the floor and turned over all of those that were facing down. He didn't think of wearing gloves.

The square pieces took some getting used to. Eight thousand one hundred and ninety pieces. Putting this picture together seemed like a hopeless venture. The only easy bit was the GLORIA IN ECCELSIS DEO banner. He was surprised by the spelling. In his state of exhaustion it was hard work to recall the text that every child used to know by heart. Glory to God in the highest . . . and peace to all men . . . of goodwill.

To prevent himself from being overwhelmed by the painful beauty of these words, he tried to add a few pieces to the banner. The electrician was making him wait. Soon, Escher felt sleep creeping into his fingers and eyes. Instead of laying the next piece of the puzzle, he lay his own heavy body on the floor covered in painted squares and waited for the electrician to ring his doorbell.

One of the real joys of my career has been the sheer diversity of the texts I have worked on: literary fiction, bloody thrillers, police procedurals, narrative histories, popular philosophies, satires, classics, and so on. With such a variety of genres and styles I try to approach each translation with an open mind, avoiding wherever possible any hard and fast rules. Over time, however, and directed largely by common sense (i.e., does that work in translation?), a few useful guidelines emerge that facilitate the translation process across all types of books.

When I embarked upon *Short Circuit*, it soon became clear that I would have to tear up my own set of personal guidelines and then burn them to a cinder. This is a playful novel: It plays with words, with the narrative, and with the reader's mind. On the one hand that provides a real translation challenge, but it is also not dissimilar to the translator's own craft. For our work is very playful too; we use smoke and mirrors in a game of deception that paradoxically strives to remain as faithful as possible to the original text.

One specific transgression in my translation of *Short Circuit* is the electrician's ringtone, which in the original German is a popular song sung in a thick Austrian accent. Ask any number of translators about accents and they'll likely give you the same answer: DON'T render them in some random English-language accent, as that DOESN'T work. They're right, it's a good piece of advice I usually adhere to. Not here. In the spirit of this impish novel I felt there was license to go rogue, and thus in the English version we have the ringtone in a cod Glaswegian accent.

I have also been pretty relaxed about leaving in the odd German and Italian word or phrase in the English translation, but only where we (myself and the editorial team) felt it was justified for the humor. In this respect the author was a great help, encouraging us to cut what didn't work rather than force something for the sake of it. Happily, this was seldom necessary; alternative jokes could often be found by playing around with the text.

Above all I allowed myself to be guided by a sense of fun. When an idea in English amused me, it generally felt right for this book. If paragraphs went by without raising a smile, I knew I had to rethink that part of the translation and approach the original with more creativity to tease out the playfulness—which made it an entertaining ride all the way.

—Jamie Bulloch

Here ends Wolf Haas's
Short Circuit.

The first edition of this book was printed
and bound at Lakeside Book Company
in Harrisonburg, Virginia, in March 2026.

A NOTE ON THE TYPE

The text of this novel was set in Bulmer MT, a typeface revival
designed by Ron Carpenter and issued by Monotype in 1930. A
transitional face that bridged the gap between "old style" and
"modern" fonts, the original Bulmer was commissioned in 1790 as
part of John Boydell's ambitious project to realize a "magnificent
and accurate" new Shakespeare edition. Today, Bulmer and its
revivals continue this storied legacy in fine printing and remain a
popular choice for historical and literary works.

HARPERVIA

An imprint dedicated to publishing international voices,
offering readers a chance to encounter other lives and other
points of view via the language of the imagination.